Goosebumps

Wailing Special

Wailing Special

Bad Hare Day
Egg Monsters From Mars
The Beast From the East

R.L. Stine

Hippo

Scholastic Children's Books,
Commonwealth House, 1–19 New Oxford Street, London, WC1A 1NU, UK
a division of Scholastic Ltd
London ~ New York ~ Toronto ~ Sydney ~ Auckland

Bad Hare Day
Egg Monsters From Mars
The Beast From the East
First published in the US by Scholastic Inc., 1996
First published in the UK as *Goosebumps Wailing Special*
by Scholastic Ltd, 1996

ISBN: 0 590 54272 9

Typeset by Rowland Phototypesetting Ltd, Bury St Edmunds, Suffolk
Printed in China

10 9 8 7 6 5 4 3 2 1

CONTENTS

CONTENTS

Goosebumps

Bad Hare Day

"Pick a card, any card." I spread out the deck of cards in front of Sue Mailer, face down. She giggled and picked one.

"Don't show it to me," I warned her. She glanced at the card, keeping it hidden from me.

A small crowd of kids gathered on the school steps to watch. School was out for the day. Sue showed them her card.

I love doing magic tricks—especially in front of an audience. My dream is to be a great magician like my idol, Amaz-O.

I've been playing around with stage names. My real name is Tim Swanson—but that's far too boring for a professional magician. I've been thinking of calling myself Swanz-O. My best friend, Foz, thinks Swanz-O sounds like a washing powder.

"Now, Sue," I said in a louder voice, so everybody could hear me. "Put the card back in the deck."

3

Sue slipped the card in with the others. I shuffled the deck and tapped it three times. "I will now make your card rise to the top of the deck," I announced.

Tap, tap, tap. I picked up the top card and showed it to Sue. "Was this your card?" I asked her.

Her eyebrows shot up in amazement. "The three of clubs!" she cried. "That was my card!"

"How'd you do that?" Jesse Brown asked.

"Magicians never reveal their secrets," I said, bowing. "And now, for my next trick—"

"I know how he did it." My little sister, Ginny, suddenly popped up in the crowd. The sound of her scratchy voice made my hair stand on end. She loves to spoil my magic shows.

But a true magician doesn't let anything throw him. I grinned my biggest, fakest grin at the little brat.

"Ladies and gentlemen, my lovely assistant, Ginny!"

"I'm not your assistant, freak-face," Ginny snarled. "You won't catch me doing nerdy magic tricks. I'm into karate. Hi-ya!" She demonstrated her karate chop.

Some of the kids laughed. I pretended to laugh, too. "Ha, ha. Isn't she a riot?"

Everybody says Ginny looks like an angel. She has long, wavy blonde hair, rosy cheeks and big blue eyes. People always ooh and aah over her.

No one ever oohs and aahs over me. I've got curly light-brown hair and hazel eyes. I'm twelve, which Mum says isn't a "cute age".

My nose is long and curves up at the end like a hot dog. Ginny likes to flick the end of my nose with her finger and say, "Boi-oi-oing."

Her nose is small and perfect, of course.

I tried to continue my show, Ginny or no Ginny. I slipped the deck of cards into my pocket and yanked out my magic scarf. "Now, be amazed as I—"

Ginny reached into my pocket and snatched out the cards. "Look, everybody!" she cried, showing them the cards. "*All* the cards are the three of clubs!"

Ginny started passing the cards around so everyone could see.

"Hey! Give those back!" I protested. I grabbed the cards away. It was true. Every single card in the deck was the three of clubs. But no one was supposed to know that.

"You're a phony," Sue mumbled.

"No—wait!" I cried. "Watch this!"

I whipped out my magic rings—two large silver hoops hooked together. The kids quietened down a little.

"These silver rings are locked together," I declared. "They're completely solid—linked together for ever!" I tugged on them to show that they wouldn't come apart.

Then I handed them to Jesse. "Try to pull the rings apart," I told him. He pulled hard. He pulled lightly. He pulled hard again. He jangled them around. The rings stayed hooked together.

I took them back. "The rings will never come apart," I said. "Unless I say the magic words." I waved one hand over the rings. "Hocus pocus!" I gently pulled the rings apart. A couple of kids clapped.

"You're not going to fall for *that* old trick, are you?" Ginny mocked. "You want to know how he does it?" She grabbed the rings away and began to demonstrate. "They're trick rings—"

"I will now make my lovely assistant disappear!" I cried, shoving Ginny aside. "Beat it!"

"Stop pushing me!" she shouted. "Hi-ya!"

She karate-kicked me in the stomach.

"Oof!" I doubled over. Everybody laughed and clapped.

"That's a great trick!" Sue said.

I clutched my stomach. Some trick.

Stupid Ginny and her karate kicks. Why did Mum have to take her to that martial-arts school? My life has been miserable ever since. She's only ten, and she fights far better than I do. I've got the bruises to show it.

"Kick him again!" somebody yelled.

Ginny crouched, ready to attack.

"Try it, and I'll tell Mum where that dent in the refrigerator door came from," I warned her.

She backed off. She knew Mum would kill her for karate-chopping the fridge just because we were out of ice-cream.

"She's not going to kick him," Jesse said. "Show's over."

The kids drifted away.

"Wait!" I cried. "Come back!"

"See you tomorrow, Tim," Sue said. Everybody began to head for home.

"Thanks for wrecking everything, Ginny," I snapped.

She flicked my nose. "Boi-oi-oing."

"Stop it!" I swatted her away. "You're definitely going to get it. I'm telling Mum about the fridge for sure."

"Go ahead," she taunted. "But if you do, I'll give you the freezer chop." She waved her arms through the air, making those weird karate noises. "*Wah wah wee—ah!* Right to the neck. You'll never walk again!"

She trotted away. "See you at home, Swanz-O!"

This is what I have to deal with every day of my life. A little sister who could kill me if she wanted to. What can I do? I'm helpless against her.

That's one reason I want to be a magician. Maybe Ginny can karate-chop my arms off—but not if I make her disappear first!

I sighed and buttoned up my denim jacket. It was almost four o'clock and getting chilly. The wind had picked up, too. When is it going to get warm? I wondered. It's the end of March—it's supposed to be spring already.

The school door burst open. "I'm outta here!" Foz shouted.

Foz's real name is Foster Martin. But he doesn't look like a Foster. He's a Foz. He's chubby, with a brown buzz cut. His shirt is always untucked.

"Where've you been?" I asked him.

"Mrs Pratt made me stay after school," he replied, making a disgusted face.

"Why?" I asked.

"No reason," Foz said.

Foz has to stay after school almost every day. He always says it's for no reason.

I picked up my magic kit and started down the school steps. Foz followed. We left the school grounds and walked towards town.

"What were *you* doing at school so late?" he asked.

"I was trying out a few magic tricks. Ginny told everybody how they work. It was a disaster."

"You need better tricks," Foz said. "Lots of kids have the same magic kit as yours."

"You're right," I agreed, rattling my kit. "This is amateur stuff. I'm ready for some *real* magic tricks. Professional ones."

"Like a hat you can pull a rabbit out of."

"Or that spinning box Amaz-O has," I added. Amaz-O was my hero—the greatest magician ever. "Did you see him on TV last week? His assistant stepped into a big black box. Amaz-O spun it around three times, and she disappeared!"

"He's doing a show at Midnight Mansion," Foz said. Midnight Mansion is a club in town where magicians perform every night.

"I know. I wish I could go. But the tickets cost twenty-five dollars."

We turned on to Bank Street and headed towards the centre of town. It wasn't on the way home, but Foz knew what I was doing. Malik's Magic Shoppe was on Bank Street. I stopped in there at least once a week, just to drool over the cool tricks they had.

"Malik's has a bunch of new tricks," I told Foz. "Designed by Amaz-O himself."

"I'll bet they're expensive," Foz said.

"They are." I reached into my pocket to see how much money I had. Five bucks.

"That'll buy you a squirting flower," Foz said. "Maybe."

I stuffed the bill back into my pocket. "You've got to see this stuff, anyway. There's a table— you put a plate or something on it—it can be anything you want. The plate will rise up over the table and float!"

"How does it work?" Foz asked.

9

"I don't know. Mr Malik wouldn't tell me. He said you have to buy the trick to find out."

"How much does it cost?"

"Five hundred dollars."

Foz rolled his eyes. "I guess you'll have to stick with card tricks."

"I guess." I sighed.

A little bell rang as we opened the door to Malik's. I breathed in the musty smell of the shop. It was jam-packed with old tricks, new tricks, magic books and costumes. There were even cages in the back for rabbits and doves. Mr Malik sold everything.

I called out, "Hi, Mr Malik." He stood behind the till. He was a short, bald old man with a fat stomach.

I waited for Mr Malik to say, "What's new, Magoo?" in his gravelly voice. That's how he greets all his regular customers.

I called out, "Hi!" again, but he didn't answer. He just stood there and grunted.

"Mr Malik?" Foz and I crept closer to the counter.

"Unh!" Mr Malik grunted. He stumbled forward.

Something was sticking out of his stomach. A sword!

"Mr Malik?" I asked. "Are you okay?"

He clutched the handle of the sword and moaned in pain.

10

Someone had stabbed him!

"Help me!" he groaned. "Please—help!"

Foz and I froze in fear. I let out a gasp—but I was too frightened to move. Foz's whole body trembled.

Mr Malik uttered another groan. Then his expression changed. He pulled out the sword— and he tossed it to me.

"Hey!" I cried. "It's a fake!"

Mr Malik laughed. He rubbed his round stomach, which hadn't been stabbed at all. "What's new, Magoo?" he chuckled. "Get a load of that trick sword. Just got it in today."

I tested the sword against my own stomach. It had a sliding blade. I pushed the blade into the handle, then let go. It popped out again. Very cool.

Foz fingered the blade. "Think of the tricks you could play on Ginny with a sword like this!"

"Like it, Tim?" Mr Malik asked. "Only twenty bucks."

I shook my head. "We're just looking, Mr Malik."

He hung the sword on the wall behind him. 'All right. Take your time and look around. But would it kill you to actually *buy* something once in a while?"

Mr Malik always said that, too.

I wandered to the back of the shop. I checked out a rack of magician's jackets. I pulled a sparkly blue dinner-jacket off the rack and tried it on. It had a trick sleeve for hiding things.

I stared at myself in the mirror. I pretended to announce myself. "The Amazing Swanz-O!"

Foz shook his head in disgust. "That name is so lame."

"Yeah, you're right." I thought of another name. "How about 'Swanson the Magnificent'?"

"It's okay," Foz said. "A little boring, but okay."

He tried on a top hat and added, "You need something cooler, like 'Tim the Destroyer'."

"That sounds like a wrestler," I commented.

"At least it's not wimpy," Foz retorted. "Like Swanz-O."

"Hey, boys." Mr Malik shuffled towards us. He held out two tickets.

"Take these, if you want them," he said. "Two free passes to Amaz-O's magic show tomorrow night."

"Wow!" I cried. I took a ticket and read it.

ADMIT ONE
AN EVENING OF MAGIC WITH THE
GREAT AMAZ-O
MARCH 23
10 P.M.
MIDNIGHT MANSION

"Thanks Mr Malik! I can't believe we'll get to see Amaz-O in person!" I gushed. "Tomorrow night!"

"Tomorrow night?" Foz frowned at his ticket. "I can't go. My aunt and uncle are coming over. It's my mother's birthday."

"So? This is a once-in-a-lifetime chance! Your mother has a birthday every year."

Foz stuffed the ticket into my palm, shaking his head. "I know my mum—and she won't see it that way. Anyway, tomorrow night is a school night."

I'd forgotten about that. I hoped my mum would let *me* go. Ten o'clock was pretty late to go out on a school night.

She has to let me go, I decided. She just *has* to. What kind of horrible mother would keep her son from seeing his hero in person? Only a really mean, monstery mother.

My mother is a grump, but she's not a monster.

I took off the blue jacket and hung it back up on the rack. A large wooden box caught my eye. It was the size of a coffin, brightly painted with red and yellow stars. I lifted the lid.

The box was empty, lined with blue velvet on the inside. "What's the box do, Mr Malik?" I asked.

"That's for sawing people in half," Mr Malik replied.

I examined the inside of the box, trying to figure out how it worked. I found no secret compartments or panels or anything.

"How does it work?" I asked Mr Malik.

"You going to buy it?" he demanded.

"Well—how much does it cost?"

"Two-fifty."

"Two dollars and fifty cents? I can afford that."

Mr Malik waved me away and started towards the stockroom at the back of the shop. "Two dollars and fifty cents," he muttered. "In your dreams."

"He meant two *hundred* and fifty dollars, Brainz-O," Foz said.

I tried to cover myself. "I knew that. I was joking."

Foz fiddled with a cool-looking trick in the corner. I moved closer to see.

"It's a guillotine," Foz said. "For chopping off heads."

The guillotine had a place for the victim to rest his head at the bottom— and a razor-sharp blade at the top.

Mr Malik emerged from the back room. "I'm closing up soon, boys," he called.

"I just want to see how this works," Foz said. He twisted a lever on the guillotine.

"Foz—no!" I cried.

The blade slid down the guillotine.

And landed with a horrifying *thunk*.

"My hand!" Foz shrieked. "My hand!"

Mr Malik gasped. "I'll call an ambulance! Nine-one-one!" He grabbed the phone.

The guillotine blade had sliced right through Foz's hand. He screamed in pain.

"Oh!" Foz moaned. "I cut off my hand!" he wailed. "I'll never write again!"

I started laughing.

"Why are you laughing?" Mr Malik demanded. "This is an emergency!"

"No, it's not." Foz held up his hands to show that he was fine. "Got a paper towel? I need to wipe off this fake blood."

"Fake?" Mr Malik stammered. "Fake blood?"

"We got you back for that sword trick," I told him.

Mr Malik clutched his sweaty forehead in his hands. "I'm so stupid! I know that's a trick guillotine. Why did I fall for such a dumb joke?"

"Hey," Foz protested. "It was a lot funnier than your sword-in-the-stomach joke."

Mr Malik wiped his brow and smiled. 'All right, boys. Enough tricks. It's five o'clock. Get out of here." He shoved us towards the door.

"Thanks for the tickets, Mr Malik," I called. "See you next week."

"Sure. Next week, when I'll have a new shipment of magic tricks you won't buy."

The bell on the door jangled as we left the shop. Foz and I walked down Bank Street towards home.

"Sure you won't go to Midnight Mansion tomorrow night?" I asked him.

"I can't. Your mum will never let you go, either."

"I'll find a way," I insisted. "You'll see."

We paused in front of Foz's house. "Come over to my house after school tomorrow," I said. "I'm giving another magic show. Only this time Ginny won't wreck it."

"I'll be there," Foz promised.

"And bring your sister's rabbit," I added.

Foz shuffled his feet uncomfortably. "Clare is not going to like that . . ." he began.

"Please, Foz," I begged. "I'm going to finish building my rabbit table tonight. The rabbit trick is going to be so amazing—"

'I'll try to bring the rabbit," Foz said. "But if anything happens to it, Clare will kill me."

"Nothing will happen to it—I promise."

I waved goodbye to Foz and went home. "The

Great Swanzini is here!" I announced as I burst into the kitchen.

"You mean the Great Jerk," Ginny mumbled. She sat at the kitchen table, folding napkins. She reached up and flicked at my nose. "Boi-oi-oing."

"Get off me." I slapped her hand away.

Mum set a plate of chicken on the table. "Go and wash, Tim," she ordered. "And tell your father supper is ready."

"Look, Mum." I held up a quarter. Then, with a flick of my wrist, I slipped it up my sleeve. "I made the quarter disappear!"

I showed her my two empty hands.

"Very nice. I see two hands that haven't been washed yet," Mum said impatiently.

"I saw the quarter go up your sleeve," Ginny sneered.

"No one appreciates me around here," I complained. "Someday I'm going to be the greatest magician in the world. And my own family doesn't care!"

Mum strode to the kitchen door. "Bill!" she called upstairs to my dad. "Supper!"

I made my way out of the kitchen to wash my hands. My parents didn't take my magic act seriously. They thought it was just a hobby.

But Ginny's karate lessons were the most important thing in the world, of course. Mum always said, "Girls need to know how to defend themselves." Now I needed to defend myself against my own sister!

I returned to the kitchen and sat down. Mum plunked a piece of chicken down beside the rice on my plate. Dad and Ginny were already eating.

"I had a terrible day at work today," Mum grumbled, ripping into her chicken. She's a high school guidance counsellor. "First Michael Lamb threatened to beat up another boy. His teacher yelled at him, and he threatened to beat her up, too. She sent him to my office. When I tried to talk to him, he said he'd beat *me* up. So I called his mother in—and *she* tried to beat me up. I had to call the police!"

"That's a piece of cake next to *my* day," Dad complained. Dad sells cars. "Some guy came in and said he wanted to test-drive the new mini-van. I handed him the keys, and he took off. He never came back. He stole the car!"

I sighed and shovelled rice into my mouth. Dinner is like this every night. Both of my parents hate their jobs.

"I had a really tough day, too," Ginny put in. "Michael Franklin teased me. So I had to karate-kick him in the leg!"

I smirked. "Poor you."

Mum's forehead wrinkled—her concerned look. "You didn't hurt yourself, did you, Ginny?"

"No," Ginny replied. "But I *could* have."

"What about me?" I protested. "*I'm* the one who got kicked in the stomach. And it hurt a lot!"

"You seem to be fine now," Dad chimed in.

I gave up. I knew that arguing would get me nowhere. Mum and Dad always take Ginny's side.

"Is there any dessert?" Ginny demanded.

"Ice-cream," Mum answered.

"I'll clear the table," I offered, hoping it would put Mum in a better mood. I needed both Mum and Dad to be in a good mood.

Because I was about to ask the big question.

Would they let me go to Midnight Mansion tomorrow night?

Would they?

I stood up, collecting dirty plates. "Guess what? Amaz-O is doing his act at Midnight Mansion tomorrow night. Mr Malik gave me two free passes." I held my breath, waiting for their answer.

"Excellent!" Ginny cried. "That means I can go too!"

"I'm not taking you," I told her. "I'll ask Mark or Jesse or somebody. Anybody but you." I dropped the plates in the sink. They crashed but didn't break.

"Careful, Tim," Mum warned.

Ginny slithered over to the sink and tried to hug me. "Please, Tim. I'm your sister. Your only sister in the whole world. I'd do *anything* for you. You have to take me with you!"

"Neither one of you is going," Dad said quietly. "It's a school night."

"But Dad, it's free!" I protested. "Just this once. Amaz-O is my hero. I'll never get another chance to see him in person!"

"What time does the show start?" Mum asked.

"Ten o'clock," I told her.

She shook her head. "Absolutely not. You're not going out at ten o'clock on a school night. Especially not to a nightclub. You're much too young." She furiously spooned ice-cream into a bowl.

"Mum—please!" I begged. "I'm twelve. I can handle it."

"You heard your mother," Dad said. "You'll have other chances to see Amaz-O, Tim. Don't worry."

Mum offered me a bowl of ice-cream. "I don't want it," I grumbled. I stormed out of the kitchen. As I left, I heard Ginny say, "Good. Now I'll get two bowls of ice-cream."

Stupid Ginny, I thought. Stupid Mum and stupid Dad. My one chance to see my idol, the great Amaz-O—and they won't let me go.

I wandered into the garage. In the corner stood a new trick I was building—the rabbit table. It was a square table that came up to my waist. The top had a hole in it that led to a secret compartment under the table.

I planned to hide a rabbit in the compartment and cover the hole with my magic top hat. When I pressed a pedal at the foot of the table, the bottom of the secret compartment would rise up. Then I'd lift my hat—and there would be the rabbit!

The table was almost finished. I turned it upside down and hammered on the bottom of the secret compartment.

This trick is going to knock everybody out tomorrow afternoon, I thought. I'll be almost as amazing as Amaz-O!

I was so busy hammering I didn't hear the garage door open. Two baby blue high-tops suddenly appeared in front of me. I didn't have to look up. I knew Ginny's smelly trainers when I saw them.

"Go away," I commanded.

She never listens to me. "You going to do the rabbit trick tomorrow?" she asked.

"Uh-huh. Now go away."

"Where are you going to get the rabbit?"

I set down my hammer. "I'm going to turn *you* into a rabbit."

"Ha ha." She flipped her wavy blonde hair. "You know what this table would be perfect for?" she asked. "Karate-chopping. I'll bet I could chop it in half with one hand."

"Try it and I'll—"

"You'll what?" she taunted.

What could I do to her? Not much. "I'll turn you into a rabbit for *real*," I threatened.

"Oh, yeah? How are you going to do that?"

"It's easy," I replied. "Mr Malik showed me how. Tonight, while you're sleeping, I'm going to sneak into your room and turn you into a rabbit."

"Give me a break," Ginny said. "That is so dumb."

"Maybe. Maybe not. I guess we'll find out tonight." I picked up my hammer again. "I hope you like carrots," I told her.

"You're crazy," she said. She hurried out of the garage.

Well, I thought. At least that got rid of her for a while.

I set the table on its legs again. All I had to do was paint it, and it would be ready.

Wouldn't it be great? I thought as I opened a can of blue paint. Wouldn't it be great if I really *could* turn Ginny into a rabbit?

But that was impossible. Wasn't it?

"We want the rabbit trick! We want the rabbit trick!"

Ginny sat in the grass in our back garden. Six or seven other kids sat around. I was in the middle of my magic act. Ginny was stirring up trouble.

She knew I didn't have a rabbit for the trick. I was still waiting for Foz to show up.

Where is he? I wondered. He's ruining my show!

The other kids joined in Ginny's chant. "The rabbit trick! The rabbit trick!"

I tried to stall them. "The amazing, incredible rabbit trick is coming up," I promised. "But first—wouldn't you like to see me pull a quarter out of Ginny's ear again?"

"No!" the kids yelled. "Boo!"

"Karate fight!" Sue called. "We want a karate fight. Ginny versus Tim!"

Things were getting ugly.

At last I glimpsed Foz at the side of the house. He waved at me frantically.

"Intermission!" I announced. "I'll be back in two minutes. And then—I'll pull a rabbit out of my hat!"

I hurried over to Foz. A big cardboard box sat at his feet.

"What took you so long?" I demanded.

"I'm sorry," Foz said. "I almost had to rip the rabbit out of Clare's hands."

I opened the box. Clare's big white rabbit lifted its nose and sniffed at me. I grabbed it and stuffed it under my jacket.

"Be careful!" Foz warned. "If anything happens to it, my sister will chop me into rabbit food!"

"The rabbit will be fine," I told him. "What could happen to it?"

I sneaked the rabbit to the table. With my back to the audience, I stuffed it into the secret compartment and plopped my hat on top.

Then I turned to face the kids. None of them had seen the rabbit. Perfect.

"Ladies and gentlemen!" I called. "Thanks for being so patient. Here is the moment you've all been waiting for—"

"Karate fight!" Ginny called.

"Even better than a karate fight!" I said. "I, the Great Timothini, will now pull a rabbit out of my hat!"

Ginny snorted. "The Great Timothini?"

I pointed at her. "You, in the front row. Quiet!"

"You be quiet!" Ginny shot back.

"Get on with it!" Jesse called.

"Okay. I need complete silence now. I must concentrate."

To my surprise, the kids actually quietened down. Even Ginny. Everyone stared up at me, waiting.

I lifted my hat off the table. "As you can see, my hat is empty. It's an ordinary, everyday top hat. Sue, will you please examine the hat?"

I passed the hat to Sue. She turned it over. "It looks like a regular hat to me," she declared.

I set the hat on the table, covering the secret compartment. "Thank you, Sue. Now—watch carefully."

I waved my arms over the hat. "Abracadabra, abracadeer, rabbit, rabbit, rabbit—*appear*!"

I stepped on the pedal to make the rabbit rise up. Then I lifted the hat with a flourish.

Nothing there. The hat stood empty.

I checked the secret compartment. No rabbit there, either.

My heart pounded. How could this be?

"The rabbit!" I cried. "It's gone!"

What have I done? I thought in horror.

My trick must have worked better than I thought!

I glanced up and saw Ginny pointing across the back garden. "There it goes!" she cried. "There's the rabbit!"

I whirled around. Clare's white rabbit was hopping away.

How could that happen? I wondered. I glanced into the secret compartment again.

I'd left one side of the secret compartment open. How could I have been so stupid?

"Tim—you promised!" Foz screamed. "Grab it!"

I chased after the rabbit. Foz huffed behind me. The rabbit had already hopped halfway across our next-door neighbours' garden. I glanced back. Ginny and the other kids were yelling and running after us.

The rabbit stopped behind a bush. I sped up— and pounced.

"Got him!" I cried. But the rabbit slipped out of my hands and bounded away.

"He's heading for the stream!" Ginny shouted.

A muddy stream ran behind all the back gardens on our block. The rabbit disappeared behind the trees that hid the stream.

Whooping like crazy, Ginny led the kids after the rabbit.

"Stop!" I yelled. "You're scaring it away!"

But none of them listened to me. There was nothing to do but keep chasing.

"Don't let the rabbit hop into the water!" Foz screamed. "He'll drown!"

"He won't drown," I told Foz. "That stream is only about two inches deep."

"Just catch the rabbit!" Foz ordered. He was in a total panic. Maybe his sister really *would* chop him into rabbit food.

The rabbit hopped through the mud and across the stream into the Darbys' garden. I shoved the other kids aside. I splashed through the stream.

The rabbit stopped. Its ears twitched.

I motioned to the others to keep still. I squatted down and crept towards the rabbit.

I saw why it had stopped. The Darbys' cat, Boo Boo, crouched low in the grass, waiting to pounce.

The rabbit was trapped between us. I crawled closer. Closer. I was almost there . . .

"Watch out for th

With a yowl, th
bounced about a f
him.

Everybody raced aft
a dirty look.

"You're ruining ever

"*You're* the one wh
place!" Foz yelled back.

"Hey!" Sue called. "Look a

Ginny had raced to the head ᴏɪ ᴛɴe pack. The rabbit paused, then started running again. Ginny took a flying leap. "*Yaw, hee ha how!*" she screeched in her weirdo karate voice.

She landed on her feet in front of the rabbit. It tried to change course. Too late.

"Hiii—ya!" Ginny swooped down and grabbed the rabbit. She held him over her head like a trophy.

"I got him!" she cried. "I got him!"

"Yay, Ginny!" Everyone crowded around her, slapping her on the back.

"Don't let him go!" Foz cried. He hurried over to Ginny and snatched the rabbit away.

We all started back to my yard. "Awesome trick, Tim." Jesse patted me on the back. "You almost made the rabbit really disappear!"

Everybody laughed. "You should change your stage name, Timothini," Sue chimed in. "How about 'The Great Goofballini'?"

he Magnificent'!" Jesse sug-

and shut my eyes. Another magic
nother disaster.

an't believe you almost lost my sister's rab-
," Foz grumbled.

"I'm sorry, Foz. I'll be more careful next time."

He clutched the rabbit tightly to his chest. "Next time, get your own rabbit."

He hurried to the side of the house and stuffed the rabbit into the box.

"Anybody want to come over to my house?" Jesse called. He lived next door. "I've got a great trick to show you—the disappearing dog. I let go of his leash, and he runs away!"

Laughing, the other kids drifted over to Jesse's house. Foz took the rabbit home to his sister.

"You going over to Jesse's?" Ginny asked.

I shook my head. "I'm going inside for a snack."

"Maybe you should do your magic act inside from now on," Ginny said. "Then your tricks won't be able to escape from you!" She giggled.

"Very funny," I mumbled. "You won't be laughing so hard when I turn *you* into a rabbit. I don't think rabbits know how to laugh."

"Ooh. I'm scared." She rolled her eyes.

"You'd better be." I leaned close to her and whispered. "Tonight's the night. Tonight, while you're sleeping, I'll turn you into a rabbit. And if you try to run away, the Darbys' cat will get you."

She rolled her eyes again. Then she reached up to tweak my nose. "Boi-oi-oing."

She trotted off to Jesse's house.

I definitely need better magic tricks, I thought as I dragged myself into the house. Better equipment, too. So I can do really *cool* tricks. Tricks that actually work.

I thought of all the stuff Mr Malik sold in his shop. If I could have just one of those tricks, I could do a great act. I've got to get one somehow.

But how?

That night everybody went to bed early. Mum and Dad were exhausted and crabby after another bad day at work.

"Today was the worst day ever!" Mum grumbled. "I'm so exhausted. Everybody to bed!"

Ginny and I knew better than to protest. We didn't want to stay up, anyway, with Mum and Dad grouching around all evening.

I lay in bed with the lights off, trying to sleep. Amaz-O's show is tonight, I thought miserably. He's performing tonight, only a few miles away from my house. I have free passes. And I can't go. It's not fair!

How am I ever going to be a great magician if I never see any magic shows? Amaz-O is the greatest of the great—and I have to miss my one chance to see him!

Or do I? A wicked thought popped into my head. Why *should* I miss the show?

I've got the tickets. I can ride to Midnight Mansion on my bike. I could sneak out of the house for a couple of hours—and Mum and Dad would never have to know.

I rolled over in bed and peered at my alarm clock. The dial glowed in the dark. Nine-forty.

The show would start in twenty minutes, I knew. I could still make it if I left right now.

I couldn't stand to think about it any longer. I had to go.

I slid out of bed, hoping my mattress wouldn't creak. I tiptoed across the room to my dressing-table. I silently pulled on a pair of jeans and a shirt.

Trainers in hand, I carefully opened my bed-room door. The house was dark. I heard Dad snoring in my parents' room down the hall.

I crept towards the stairs. Am I really doing this? I thought, suddenly nervous. Am I really sneaking out in the middle of the night to go to Midnight Mansion?

Yes—I'm really doing it, I thought. I'll do *any-thing* to see Amaz-O. It's totally worth the risk.

What's the worst that could happen?

Mum and Dad could find out. Then what? Maybe they'd ground me. But I will have seen the great Amaz-O in person. And while I'm grounded, I can try to learn some of Amaz-O's tricks.

Anyway, I won't get caught. I won't.

I paused at the top of the stairs. The stairs in my house are the creakiest stairs in the universe.

Once when I was little, I tried to sneak downstairs on Christmas Eve to see what Santa had left me. I barely touched the top step with my foot—*CRRREEEEAAAK!* Mum burst out of her room before I even had a chance to try the second step.

It's not going to happen this time, I told myself. I'll take each step very slowly. I'll lean on the banister to keep them from creaking. No one will wake up. No one will hear me.

I put both my hands on the banister and rested my weight on it. Then I set my right foot carefully—the toe, then the heel—on the top step.

Crick. Just a tiny little sound. I'm sure no one heard it, I thought.

I shifted my hands down the banister and took another step. This one made no creak at all.

So far, so good.

I took a third step. *Creak*. Not a rip-roaring loud creak, but louder than the first. I froze.

I listened for the sound of someone stirring in the house.

Silence. All clear.

If Amaz-O only knew what I'm going through to see him, I thought. I must be his biggest fan on the face of the earth.

I made it all the way down the stairs with only one more creak. I breathed a sigh of relief.

I'm safe now, I thought. I'll wait until I get outside to put my shoes on. Then I'll grab my bike and go.

I tiptoed across the cold hallway floor. I reached for the handle of the front door. Twisted it.

Almost there.

Almost.

Then a shrill voice demanded, "Tim—where do you think you're going?"

I spun around. Ginny!

She was dressed in jeans and a sweater, all ready to go out. She bounded down the stairs.

"Ssshhhhhhhh! You'll wake up Mum and Dad!"

I grabbed her by the arm and yanked her out of the front door.

"What are you doing up?" I demanded.

"I was waiting for you to come into my room and turn me into a rabbit," she replied. "Or pretend to, anyway."

"I'm not going to do that tonight," I said. "Go back to bed."

"What are *you* doing up? Where are you going?"

I sat on the front steps and pulled on my trainers. "Out to the garage," I lied. "To practise a new trick."

"You are not. I know where you're going. To Midnight Mansion!"

I grabbed her by the shoulders. "Okay. You're

right. I'm going to Midnight Mansion. Don't tell Mum and Dad—promise?"

"I want to go!" she insisted. "Let me go with you."

"No. Go back to bed—and don't tell. Or you'll be sorry."

"You *have* to take me!" she declared. "If you don't, I'll run upstairs and tell Mum and Dad right now. Then you'll never get to see Amaz-O."

"You wouldn't."

"I would."

I knew she would.

"All right," I agreed. "You can come. But you have to be good and do everything I tell you to do."

"Maybe I will—and maybe I won't."

I sighed. I had to take her, no matter how bratty she was. If I did, she'd never tell— because then she'd be in as much trouble as me.

"Let's go," I whispered.

We sneaked into the garage and got our bikes. Then we pedalled off into the night.

It felt strange riding down Bank Street late at night. The shops were all closed and dark. Hardly any traffic on the street.

Oh, no. A police car up ahead—cruising towards us down Bank Street. If he spotted us, he'd stop us for sure. And then he'd take us home. And then we'd *really* be in trouble.

I searched desperately for a place to hide. The

police couldn't miss us—Bank Street was lined with streetlights.

"Ginny!" I called. "Quick—out of the light!" I swerved into the dark doorway of a dress shop. Ginny followed. We leaped off our bikes and pressed ourselves into the shadows.

The police car glided past. I held my breath as the headlights brushed across us. The car stopped.

"He saw us!" Ginny whispered. "Run!"

I grabbed her arm to stop her. "Wait." I peeked out into the street.

The police car was idling, but the driver stayed inside.

"It's a red light," I told Ginny. A few seconds later the light turned green, and the police car rolled away.

"We're safe now," I said. We hopped back on to our bikes and rode off.

Midnight Mansion loomed huge and dark at the edge of town. People said that a crazy old woman had lived alone in the mansion for forty years. She was rich, but so stingy she wore ragged old clothes and ate nothing but peanut butter, right out of the jar.

When people tried to visit her, she screamed, "Go away!" and threw rocks at them. She had about fifty cats. When she died, a businessman bought the mansion and turned it into a nightclub.

I braked in front of the old house and stared at it. Midnight Mansion.

It looked like a spooky old castle made of sooty black stone. Three storeys tall, with two towers shooting up into the night sky. Vines crept across the roof. A floodlight threw creepy shadows over the house.

I'd seen the mansion a million times before. But late at night it looked bigger and darker than usual. I thought I saw bats fluttering around the two towers.

"No wonder the old lady went crazy," Ginny whispered. "Living in a spooky place like that."

"Do you think she kept prisoners in those towers?" I wondered.

"I think she had a torture chamber in the basement," Ginny said.

We walked our bikes up to the entrance. People hurried inside to see Amaz-O's magic show. Three men in long black capes breezed past us. A woman with long black hair, black lipstick and pointy black fingernails smiled at me.

"Where did all these weird people come from?" Ginny asked.

I shrugged. "Let's go in. The show is about to start."

We locked our bikes and ran up the long stone steps. We entered a big hall lit by a crystal chandelier. We crossed the hall to a doorway covered by a heavy red curtain.

A tall, thin man in a black dinner-jacket guarded the curtain. He reached out a long, bony finger to stop us.

He had no hair, a pencil neck and dark, hollow eye sockets. "He looks like a skeleton," Ginny whispered to me.

I pulled the two tickets out of my back pocket and handed them to him.

"Very good," he croaked in a low voice. "But where are your parents? I can't seat children without their parents."

My parents? Think fast, Swanz-O, I told myself. "Um—my parents. Yes. Well, my parents, you see . . ." I had a feeling he didn't want to hear that my parents were at home sleeping.

"They're outside, parking the car," I lied. "They'll be here in a minute. They told us to come in and get a table."

The man's hollow black eyes seemed to burn a hole in my brain. Would he buy it?

"I don't like it. But all right." He led us through the red curtain. The houselights went down just as we walked in. He showed us to a table right next to the stage.

"Excellent!" I said to Ginny as we sat down. "The best seats in the whole place!"

"This is so exciting!" she exclaimed. "I can't believe we're in a real, grown-up nightclub. By ourselves!"

The eerie-looking host stood by the red curtain, watching us. "We may not be here long," I warned her. "That skeleton guy's got his eye on us. When he realizes we're not here with our parents—"

"Shh! The show's starting."

A voice came over a loudspeaker. "Ladies and gentlemen! Midnight Mansion is proud to present the most famous magician in America. The fabulous, the incredible, the mind-boggling Amaz-O!"

A drum roll, and then horns bleating. "Ta da!" The audience clapped and cheered. The curtain rose.

I gasped when I saw the stage. It was filled with wonderful equipment—a tall, shiny black box with a door in the front, a platform suspended from the ceiling, a glittering box with holes in it for a head, arms and legs to stick out of. And a big white rabbit sitting beside a vase of blue flowers on a table covered with a red scarf.

The rabbit wasn't tied up or caged or anything. "I wonder how he keeps that rabbit from running away," Ginny whispered. "That's a trick *you* need to learn."

"You're so funny, Ginny," I said, rolling my eyes. "My sides are splitting with laughter."

"You have no sense of humour," Ginny jeered. "That's your problem."

"No. *You're* my problem," I snapped.

Amaz-O strode on stage. He was tall and slim, and his top hat made him seem even taller. He had long black hair and wore a black cape lined with red satin over a black dinner-jacket.

He tossed the cape over his shoulders and bowed.

I can't believe I'm seeing Amaz-O in person! I thought, my heart pounding with excitement. And so close—I could almost touch him!

Maybe I'll even see how some of his tricks are done, I thought. Maybe, sitting so close, I'll catch some of his secrets!

Without saying a word, Amaz-O scanned the audience. He trained his eyes on me.

My whole body shook. He's staring right at me! I gasped.

Amaz-O took a step forward and leaned towards me.

What's he doing? I thought. Is he going to talk to me?

Amaz-O leaned closer. His face was right next to mine! I cowered in my seat.

He scowled and whispered in a deep, menacing voice, "Disappear! Disappear!"

I shrank back.

"Disappear!" he growled again.

"Excuse me?" I gasped. I stared up at him. On TV he seemed friendly. But in person he was definitely frightening.

"Disappear!" he whispered. "I'm going to make you disappear at the end of the show. I will ask for volunteers—and I will choose you."

He didn't want me to disappear for real. He wanted me to be part of his act! I couldn't believe it!

I'll find out how he does his famous disappearing trick! I thought. Maybe I'll get to meet him after the show. Maybe he'll even tell me some of his secrets!

Ginny leaned across the table. "He's going to make you disappear for ever!" she teased. "What will I tell Mum and Dad?"

I paid no attention to her. Nothing Ginny did or said could bother me now.

This was too cool! Just seeing Amaz-O was exciting enough. But he chose *me* to be in his show!

Maybe he could tell that I'm a magician, too, I thought.

Amaz-O began his act. "Good evening, ladies and gentlemen," he crooned. "Tonight you will see some amazing feats. You will see me do things you always thought were impossible. Are these feats real—or are they illusions? It's up to you to decide."

He waved his hands, and a wand appeared out of thin air. The audience clapped.

Then Amaz-O began to fidget with his hat, as if it felt uncomfortable on his head. "Something is wrong with my hat," he said. "It feels strange—almost as if . . ."

He lifted the hat off his head and peered into it. He showed us the inside of it. It looked perfectly normal. There was nothing inside it.

He placed it back on his head. "It's funny," he chuckled. "I thought for a minute there might be something inside my hat. I thought I felt—oh, I don't know—a flock of birds fluttering around in there."

The hat jiggled. Amaz-O appeared annoyed. "There it goes again!"

He whipped the hat off his head and stared into it. On top of his head sat a large white feather. People in the audience giggled.

"What's so funny?" Amaz-O asked. He felt the top of his head and found the feather. "Where did that come from?" he gasped, acting amazed. Everyone laughed.

"Well, I'll try not to let this bother me," he went on, replacing his hat. "Back to the show. For my first trick—"

The hat began to shake again—slightly at first, then harder. It practically jumped off his head. The audience cracked up. Amaz-O pretended to be horrified.

He yanked the hat off his head—and out flew a whole flock of doves! They swooped over the audience and flew up to the rafters.

"I *knew* something was going on in there!" Amaz-O joked. Loud laughter and clapping.

He's the greatest, I thought, clapping along. How did he get all those birds inside his hat?

I glanced at the rabbit on stage. It sat calmly on the table, staring at Amaz-O. It almost seemed to be watching the act.

I can't wait to see his rabbit trick, I thought. Will he make the rabbit disappear? Or pull off some kind of twist?

"For my next trick I need a needle and thread," Amaz-O announced. He produced a packet of needles and a long, thick thread from one of his pockets. He picked out a needle and squinted, trying to push the thread through the eye.

"I always have trouble threading a needle," he said. He licked the end of the thread and tried again. He couldn't get the thread to go through.

He threw up his hands in frustration. "It's impossible!" he cried. "How do tailors do it?"

The audience chuckled. I waited to see what would come next. I knew all this needle-and-thread business was a build-up to something incredible.

"So much for the *hard* way to thread a needle," Amaz-O said. "I'll show you a better way."

He snatched up the packet of needles. There must have been at least twenty needles stuck into a piece of cardboard. He popped the whole thing into his mouth. Then he dangled the long string over his mouth like a piece of spaghetti.

He slowly drew the string into his mouth, chewing. It looked as if he were eating a piece of spaghetti—with a packet of needles in his mouth, too.

"Don't you think that hurts?" Ginny whispered. "Chewing up all those needles?"

I barely nodded. I watched Amaz-O, spellbound.

Amaz-O nearly swallowed the whole string. About an inch of string stuck out between his lips. The audience waited, hushed.

He paused. Then he opened his mouth and tugged at the string. Slowly, slowly, he pulled it out of his mouth.

One by one the needles appeared—dangling from the string! Somehow he had threaded twenty needles with his tongue!

The audience gasped, then applauded. The needles flashed as Amaz-O held up the string.

"Threading needles the easy way!" he cried as he took another bow.

I've got to find out how he did that, I thought. Maybe I'll ask him after the show.

"How's the show going?" Amaz-O asked the audience. We all cheered. "I wonder how much time we have left?" He strode across the stage to the table where the rabbit and the blue flowers sat on top of the red scarf.

With a flick of his wrist, he yanked his scarf out from under the rabbit.

The rabbit didn't move. Neither did the vase of flowers. The table was now bare.

The rabbit blinked calmly. Amaz-O waved the scarf over his left hand. He let it drop—and a big red alarm clock appeared in his hand!

He glanced at the clock. "I suppose we have time for a few more tricks." He covered the clock with the scarf—and the clock disappeared.

A loud ringing suddenly erupted from the other side of the stage. I turned towards it.

The red alarm clock—floating in mid-air! It seemed to have flown across the stage by itself.

Amaz-O crossed the stage, grabbed the clock, and shut off the alarm.

"My clock is a little fast," he joked. "It's not time for the show to end. Not yet."

I hope not, I thought. This is the greatest magic act I've ever seen in my life!

The rest of the show was fantastic, too. Amaz-O escaped from a locked safe. He walked through a brick wall. He tapped his hat with his magic wand—and in a puff of smoke his dinner-jacket changed from black to yellow!

"And now for my big finale," Amaz-O announced. "I am going to make a member of the audience disappear. Are there any volunteers?"

He gazed out over the audience. No one said a word. Ginny kicked me under the table.

"Ow!" I whispered, rubbing my skin. "What did you do that for?"

"He asked for *volunteers*, you moron," she said. "That means you."

I'd been so caught up in the show, I almost forgot. I stood up. "I'd like to volunteer."

Amaz-O smiled. "Excellent, young man. Please step up on stage."

My stomach suddenly jolted with terror. I stumbled up to the stage.

Here I go, I thought nervously. Amaz-O is going to make me disappear.

I hope nothing goes wrong.

Amaz-O towered over me on stage. This is un-
believable, I thought. I'm on stage with the great
Amaz-O. I'm about to be part of one of his
famous tricks.

He's going to make me disappear!

I clutched my stomach, wondering, why do I
feel so scared?

"Thanks for volunteering, young man,"
Amaz-O said to me. "You must be very brave.
Are your parents here tonight?"

My parents? Uh-oh. "Um—they're here. Sure
they're here," I stammered. "But—uh—they
had to make a phone call."

Amaz-O frowned. "A phone call? In the middle
of my show?"

"Well—it was an emergency," I explained.

"Never mind. I'm glad they've stepped away.
If they knew what was about to happen to you,
they might try to stop me."

"Stop you?" My heart skittered nervously. But I heard the audience laughing.

Don't let him scare you, I told myself. This is just part of the act. He's joking.

I faked a laugh. "What—um—exactly—is about to happen to me?"

"I'm going to make you disappear," Amaz-O replied. "You will be transported into another dimension. I will try my best to bring you back, of course—but it doesn't *always* work."

"It doesn't?" I gulped.

He patted me on the back. "Don't worry. I've done this hundreds of times. I've only missed once or twice."

The audience chuckled. They figured he was kidding. I hoped they were right.

"Is that your sister sitting at the front table?" Amaz-O asked.

I nodded.

"Better wave goodbye to her, just in case," he warned me.

Ginny smiled and waved at me.

She can't *wait* for me to disappear! I thought bitterly. She hopes I'll never come back.

"Go on," Amaz-O urged. "Wave to her."

I smiled weakly and waved at Ginny. The audience laughed. Then Amaz-O led me to a tall black box in the centre of the stage. He threw open the door. It looked like a cupboard inside.

"Step inside here if you would, please," he said.

I stepped inside the box. Amaz-O shut the door firmly.

It was pitch-black inside that box. I stood still, waiting for something to happen. I could hear Amaz-O talking to the audience.

"Ladies and gentlemen, this box is my own invention—the Fifth Dimension Spin-o-Rama." I heard him slap his hand against the side of the box.

"Here's how it works: my brave volunteer steps inside the box. I lock him in. I spin the box ten times—*very* fast.

"A magical force inside the box will send the boy into another dimension. He will disappear!

"I must ask for absolute silence while I do this trick. I need complete concentration."

For several seconds I heard nothing.

Then the box began to spin. "Whoa!" I cried. My body slammed against the back of the box.

It whirled around faster than any ride in an amusement park. I shut my eyes. I felt so dizzy.

I hope I don't puke, I thought. That would spoil everything.

The box kept spinning, spinning. How will the trick work? I wondered. How will I disappear?

What if he really sends me into another dimension?

But that's just talk, I told myself. Magician talk—to entertain the audience.

Isn't it?

The box spun faster and faster. I clutched my stomach. I saw stars dancing before my eyes.

When is it going to stop? I thought. I'm really going to be sick.

Then, suddenly, the bottom of the box dropped out from under me.

"Help!" I cried as I fell down, down, down.

"Whoa!"

I slid down a long wooden chute and landed— *thunk!*—on some kind of mattress.

I lay on my back in a daze. I heard water dripping somewhere. A dim yellow light flickered from a bare bulb on the ceiling.

I sat up, gazing around me. The room was nearly empty, dark and damp, with a cement floor. I spotted a furnace in the corner.

I'm in the basement of Midnight Mansion, I realized.

I stood up and examined the chute. So that's how the trick works, I thought. Amaz-O sets up his spinning box over a trapdoor in the floor of the stage. The bottom of the box drops out, and the volunteer slides down the chute and out of sight. When Amaz-O opens the door of the box— *presto!*—the volunteer has disappeared. It's so simple.

But how do I get back upstairs? I wondered. How will Amaz-O make me reappear?

Muffled applause drifted down from overhead. I could hear Amaz-O's voice, faintly. "Thank you very much, ladies and gentlemen. I must be going now. I've got to disappear into the fifth dimension and find that boy! Good night!"

The audience laughed. Then I heard music, an explosion, and loud clapping.

Amaz-O must have made himself disappear, I thought. He'll probably come sliding down this chute any minute.

I waited.

No one came sliding down the chute.

I waited a few more minutes.

Nothing.

He must have disappeared some other way, I figured.

He'll show up soon, I thought. He'll come and let me out of here. And then I'll ask him how he does that trick with the alarm clock. Maybe he'll even give me his autograph!

A few minutes later I heard chairs scraping across the floor upstairs and a stampede of footsteps. The show was over. The audience was leaving.

Is somebody going to let me out of here? I wondered. I was getting a little nervous. I sat down on the mattress to wait.

What's taking Amaz-O so long?

Maybe he wants to wait until everyone is gone, so no one will figure out how he did the trick. That must be it.

I waited a little longer. I heard a rustling, scuttling noise. A rat! I thought, jumping up off the mattress. I stared at the floor, watching for the rat.

The noise stopped.

Maybe it wasn't a rat, I thought, trying to calm myself. My muscles were all tense. Maybe it was only a mouse. Or a cockroach. Or my imagination.

The *drip, drip, drip* of the water somewhere in the basement was starting to drive me crazy. *Drip, drip, drip*. Like some kind of water torture.

Where is Amaz-O? When is he going to let me out of here?

I listened for signs of life upstairs. Nothing. Everything was silent up there now.

Okay, I said to myself. Everyone is gone. You can let me out now, Amaz-O.

I listened hard. I didn't hear anyone in the building.

What if Amaz-O is gone, too? I thought, panicking. What if he's forgotten about me and left me here?

I've got to find a way out myself, I decided.

I crept across the cement floor, keeping an eye out for rats.

It sure is dark down here, I thought.

I drifted towards the dripping sound and found myself in a room with a big laundry sink. I crossed the laundry room. On the other side I found a steep flight of steps leading to a door at the top.

Aha, I thought, feeling better now. A way out.

I climbed the rickety stairs. I reached for the doorknob and pushed.

The door didn't open. I turned the knob again and pulled.

Nothing.

The door was locked!

I rattled the door as hard as I could. I pounded on it with my fists.

"Let me out of here!" I cried. "Can anyone hear me?

"Let me out of here!"

"Hey!" I shouted. I rattled the door. "Somebody! Get me out of here!"

How could Amaz-O do this? I thought angrily. How could he forget all about me like this?

He wouldn't lock me in the basement on purpose—would he?

No, I told myself. Why would he want to do that?

It's all just a big mistake.

I shook the door again. It loosened a little. I pushed on it, and it opened a crack.

The door was bolted from the outside with a metal hook. But the hook wasn't secure.

I'll bet I can break the door open, I realized.

I backed part of the way down the stairs. Then I ran to the top and threw myself against the door.

"Ow!" I grunted. The door loosened a little more. But it didn't open. And now my shoulder ached.

Then I thought the unthinkable. I couldn't believe I was thinking this—but I sure wished Ginny were with me.

She could've karate-kicked through that door in about five seconds. I know, because she's kicked her way into my bedroom lots of times.

Where is Ginny, anyway? I thought. She must be outside in the car park, waiting for me.

I had to try again. I rammed my shoulder against the door as hard as I could.

Bang! The hook broke, and the door flew open.

Excellent, I thought, rubbing my shoulder. I'm out of that horrible basement at last.

But where am I now?

A long, dark corridor.

"Hello?" I called. No answer. "Hello?"

Where is everybody? I wondered. Shouldn't there be stage-hands bustling around or something?

I tiptoed down the hall. The place appeared deserted.

How could they have left me down in the basement like that? I thought angrily. How could they leave me here alone—and just go home?

At the end of the hall I saw a sliver of light. It came from under a door.

Someone's still here, I realized. Maybe it's Amaz-O!

I crept down the hall. The door had a star on it. It must be Amaz-O's dressing room! I thought. This is fantastic! I'm alone in Midnight Mansion with the great Amaz-O! We'll probably stay up all night talking about magic. If I could get him to show me a few of his secrets . . .

I felt so excited and nervous my hands shook. I almost forgot about being left in the basement.

That was just a mistake, I thought. A stage-hand forgot to come and get me. Amaz-O must have thought I was all right. He'll probably be really glad to see me.

I stared at the star on the door. What should I do? I wondered. Should I knock? Should I call out his name?

I'll knock, I decided. I stepped to the door. *Thunk!* I tripped over something propped against the wall. A large black case with PROPERTY OF AMAZ-O written on the side.

Wow, I thought, running my fingers along the gold letters. This must be Amaz-O's magic kit! I'm touching it with my own hands!

I turned back to the door. I was about to meet my idol, my all-time hero. It was the biggest moment of my life.

I reached for the door. My hand trembled. I knocked lightly.

I waited.

Maybe he didn't hear me, I thought. I knocked again, harder this time.

Nothing.

"Hello?" I called softly, peeking into the room.

Amaz-O's big white rabbit perched on the couch. Amaz-O sat on a chair across from the rabbit. I could see his legs.

"Hello?" I called again. "It's me. From the disappearing act. Can I come in?"

I paused at the door. Amaz-O didn't answer me. Suddenly the door slammed shut in my face!

"Hey!" I cried in surprise.

A voice growled at me from the other side. "Beat it!"

"But—I'm your biggest fan! I'd just like to shake hands—"

"Beat it!" the voice snarled again. "Beat it, punk!"

Punk? *Punk?*

Did the great Amaz-O call me a punk?

I couldn't believe it. I stood staring at the star on the door in shock.

How could Amaz-O talk to me this way? After I volunteered for his disappearing trick—and he left me locked in the basement!

What's his *problem*, anyway?

For a few seconds I couldn't move. I couldn't think. My hero had called me a punk. The greatest magician in the world—and he turned out to be a big fat jerk!

Okay, so he wasn't fat. But he was the biggest jerk I'd ever met in my whole life.

I hung my head and turned away from the door to leave. Then I saw it again—the big black case.

Amaz-O's magic kit.

Without thinking, I grabbed the case and ran. It was heavy and awkward, but I lugged it down the hall as quickly and quietly as I could.

Why am I doing this? I wondered as I burst into the stage area.

I'm still not sure why I did it. I'd gone through so much trouble to get to the show—sneaking out of the house to meet Amaz-O. And then he was so mean to me. Maybe I wanted to get back at him.

It doesn't matter why I did it. I did it. I stole Amaz-O's magic tricks.

In the back of my mind, I knew I was heading for trouble.

I paused near the stage. Was Amaz-O following me? I listened.

Not a sound. No one coming. I swallowed hard and started running again.

I passed under the chandelier in the lobby and burst through the front door. I hope Amaz-O was the last person in the club, I thought. I hope there aren't any guards lurking around.

I didn't have time to check. I dragged the case across the gravel car park towards my bike.

Almost there, I told myself, panting. The car park was empty now. The floodlights that lit up the mansion were off. The old house lay hidden in darkness.

It must be really late, I thought. I'd better hurry home.

My bike stood where I'd left it, leaning against a rail.

I was reaching for the handlebars when a voice called, "Stop!"

I froze.

I knew I was caught.

I heard heavy footsteps crunch towards me across the gravel car park.

Here they come, I thought. They've caught me red-handed with Amaz-O's bag. They'll probably arrest me.

"Where were you?" the voice called.

Ginny! I'd completely forgotten about her. Oops.

"Why are you leaving without me?" she demanded.

"Wh-why?" I stammered. What could I say? I didn't want to admit I'd forgotten all about her. "I-I wasn't leaving without you. I was looking for you. Where have *you* been?"

"Looking for *you*, Tim," she snapped. "What happened to you? You disappeared—and you never came back!"

"It's a long story," I said.

She leaned forward to read the lettering on

Amaz-O's black case. "'Property of Amaz-O.' Where did you get that?"

"He gave it to me," I lied. "Wasn't that nice of him?"

She reached out to open the clasp that held the case shut. "Cool. What's inside?"

I stopped her hand. "I'll show it to you when we get home. It's filled with tricks. Amaz-O said I could keep it. He was grateful to me for being such a good sport in the disappearing act."

Ginny looked puzzled. "If Amaz-O gave you that case," she began, "why are those guards running this way?"

I glanced towards the mansion. Two guards charged across the car park, waving torches. Uh-oh.

I grabbed the case. "Let's get out of here!" I cried. "Quick—get on your bike. Let's ride!"

"I can't!" Ginny cried.

"Huh? Why not?"

"My bike's gone!"

I jumped on my bike. "Too bad!" I cried. "See you at home!"

"Tim!" Ginny wailed. "You can't leave me here!"

I would have left her there if I could. She can take care of herself. But I knew Mum and Dad would kill me.

Besides, when the guards caught her, she'd tell on me. I'd still get in trouble.

I sat on my bike, watching the guards run right for us. Then I spotted her bike on the edge of the car park. "It's over there!" I told her. "Hurry!"

She raced to her bike. I balanced the case on top of my handlebars. It wasn't easy.

"Stop!" a guard yelled. Ginny and I sped out of the car park and down the dark street.

"Hey—stop!" the guards shouted. The beams of their torches blinded me for a second. I pedalled as hard as I could. Ginny darted ahead of me.

I clutched the black case with one hand and steered with the other. The case slowed me down. The guards were gaining on us. At the first corner I zoomed left. Ginny followed.

I glanced back. The guards had stopped running. One of them bent over, panting.

"They'll never catch us now!" Ginny shouted. We biked home as fast as we could. The streets were empty and really dark. The lights were out in most of the houses.

It's after midnight, I realized. Please let Mum and Dad be asleep. If they catch us, they'll ground us till we're thirty-five! I'd almost rather be arrested.

But then, if I got arrested, Mum and Dad would *still* ground me.

We braked at our street and walked our bikes into the driveway.

"Sshhh," Ginny whispered.

"Sshhh yourself," I whispered back.

We parked the bikes in the garage. It was hard to see without the lights on. On the way into the house, Ginny tripped over the lawn mower.

"Ow!" she yelped.

"Quiet!" I snapped.

We both froze. Did Mum and Dad hear us? Silence. "I think it's okay," I whispered.

"That hurt," Ginny whined.

"Ssshhhh!"

We sneaked into the house. "I'll hide the case in my room," I whispered.

"I want to look at it now," Ginny protested.

I shook my head. "It's mine."

"No, it's not. You have to share it with me."

"Amaz-O gave it to *me*," I insisted, even though it wasn't exactly true.

"I'm going to tell Mum and Dad," Ginny threatened. "I'll tell them you woke me up and forced me to go with you to Midnight Mansion."

"You little brat!" I cried angrily. Stupid Ginny. "Okay, I'll share it with you."

"Promise?"

"If you promise not to tell Mum and Dad."

"I promise. But you can't keep the case in your room. It's both of ours now."

I sighed. "All right. I'll hide it in the attic. Okay?"

She nodded.

"But we won't touch it until Saturday," I said. "On Saturday, we'll have plenty of time to try everything out and do it right. Deal?"

"Deal. On Saturday we'll *both* open the case, at the same time, *together*."

"Right. Now go to bed. I'll sneak it up to the attic."

We tried to be careful going up the creaky stairs. It took us about ten minutes. At the top

I paused to listen for sounds from Mum and Dad's room.

"Everything is okay," Ginny whispered. "Dad is snoring."

She crept into her room and shut the door. I tiptoed up to the attic, lugging the black case.

I shut the attic door and switched on the light. Where can I hide this? I wondered, gazing around at all the junk. I stepped over piles of old magazines. In one corner sat my old toy chest.

Perfect, I thought, opening the chest. I pulled out a toy school bus and a couple of trucks to make room for the case.

What's in here, anyway? I wondered as I hefted Amaz-O's case. I held Amaz-O's magic kit in my hands. How could I go to sleep without seeing what's in it? How could I wait two whole days until Saturday?

Maybe I'll take a little peek inside, I thought. Just a quick one. Then I'll go to bed.

I set the case on the floor. My hands trembled as I fumbled with the clasp.

Here goes, I thought, tugging open the clasp. I pulled the case open—

And it blew up in my face!

I fell over backwards. I lay sprawled on the floor, covering my eyes.

What happened?

Am I dead?

I opened my eyes. I squeezed my arms. I grabbed my chest.

I'm okay, I realized.

I sat up. The case sat on the floor. No signs of an explosion.

Carefully I crawled over to the case. I could have sworn it had blown up. But I didn't see anything that would blow up.

Then, taped to the inside of the top flap, I saw a little metal disk. I tapped it. It made a muffled roar.

I examined the metal disk. It was an electronic chip. It made an explosion sound effect when I shook it or tapped it.

Just one of Amaz-O's tricks.

What else is in here? I wondered.

I pulled out all kinds of cool stuff. A pair of trick handcuffs. A pocket watch for hypnotizing people. Three different packs of trick cards. A rope. And a long chain of silk scarves tied together.

I wonder how all this stuff works, I thought. I'll have to fool around with it on Saturday and figure it out.

I found a small black sack that held three oval shells and a little red ball. The shell game, I realized. One of my favourite tricks. You hide the ball under one of the shells and shift them around. The audience has to guess which shell the ball is under.

They always guess wrong, because the ball isn't under *any* of the shells. The magician secretly palms the ball while he's shifting the shells around.

Gets 'em every time.

I reached into the case again. My hand brushed against something silky. I pulled it out. It was a black dinner-jacket.

"Wow!" I gasped. "Amaz-O's own jacket!"

I had to try it on. I pulled it over my shoulders. It was too big. The shoulders drooped halfway down my arms, and the sleeves covered my hands.

But it felt great. I ran my hands over the satin lapels.

I stood up and walked around in it. A real

magician's jacket. I wonder what he's got in the pockets?

I stuck my hands in the pockets. But suddenly I felt something wiggle. Along the back of the jacket, near the neck.

I shook my shoulders. The wiggling stopped.

But then I felt it again. Something came sliding down the sleeve!

I shook my arm. What is it? I thought. Is it alive?

The thing crawled along my arm. "Yuck!" I sputtered. "Get off me!" I squirmed inside the coat, trying to shake the thing off.

I had to get the jacket off—straight away! I struggled to get my arms out of the sleeves.

Then something poked its head out. Out of the sleeve, near my hand.

A snake.

A live snake.

16

I clamped my mouth shut to keep from screaming. The snake felt warm and creepy against my arm. I shook my arm hard. The snake clung to me!

I gritted my teeth and shook my arm again. And again. I brushed at my sleeve with my free hand.

It wasn't working!

I shook my arm once more, as hard as I could. The snake uncoiled and slithered out of the sleeve. It dropped to the floor.

It hissed and curved around the toy chest. I watched it with a shiver.

Then I felt it again—that slippery, wriggling feeling. Something hissed near my ear and squirmed across my shoulder.

"Ohhh!" I moaned. Another snake! I slapped at it. "Get off me!"

As I tried to brush the snake away, another one slithered down my sleeve. Something slimy wriggled across my stomach and down my back. A snake popped out of an inner pocket and plopped to the floor. It started to coil around my leg.

The jacket is crammed with snakes! I realized with horror.

I thrashed my arms, frantically trying to tear off the jacket. A snake slid down the front of my shirt.

I thrashed harder, shaking my arms and legs. Now I was covered with snakes! My whole body!

I wanted to scream—but I couldn't wake Mum and Dad. A snake curled up my neck and around my head. I squirmed, desperately trying to get out of the jacket.

"Help!" I moaned. "Ohhhh—help!"

Snakes everywhere!

One slithered over my head. With a trembling hand, I grabbed at it and heaved it away.

Gasping in terror, I struggled out of the jacket. I tossed it on the floor. Snakes wriggled over it. Snakes wriggled over my feet. I hopped up and down. Then I hopped on to a chair. A snake coiled up the leg of the chair. It crept closer. "Go away!" I whispered. "Leave me alone!"

The snake hissed. I jumped off the chair.

Squish! My stomach turned. Did I step on a snake? I was afraid to look.

I lifted my foot and glanced down. I hadn't stepped on a snake. It was one of Ginny's old dolls.

A snake slid over the doll's face and around its neck. Another snake slithered over my shoe.

There's no escape! I realized. I've got no

choice—I have to wake up Mum and Dad. What else can I do?

I hopped around the squirming, hissing snakes. I'll get into trouble, I thought. But at least I'll be out of this snake pit!

A snake darted towards me—then suddenly froze. The room fell silent. No more hissing.

All around me the snakes stopped moving. They lay stiff on the floor. Their cold eyes stared.

What happened? Were they dead?

I glanced around, afraid to move. The floor was littered with dead snakes.

How could they all die at once? I wondered. It's so weird!

I stood there, not moving a muscle. My eyes darted around the room.

I slowly reached out my leg and tapped one of the snakes with my foot. It jiggled a little.

I took a deep breath. Should I touch it?

I got up the courage to bend close to the snake. I stuck out a finger and poked at it. Nothing happened. My heart pounded. I picked up the snake.

It lay limp in my hand. It didn't seem real.

I twisted the body. It was rubber! I examined the eyes. They were made of glass.

They're mechanical snakes, I realized.

I turned the snake over. I found a tiny wind-up key hidden under a rubber flap.

Amaz-O's jacket was rigged with wind-up snakes.

I began to breathe again. Everything is okay, I told myself. I don't have to wake up Mum and Dad. I'm not going to get into trouble. I'm not going to be eaten alive by snakes.

When will I learn? I scolded myself. *All* of these things are just tricks. None of them is real. Amaz-O is a magician.

I gathered up the snakes and stuffed them back inside the jacket. Then I jammed the jacket into Amaz-O's magic kit. I took one last look inside the bag.

This is amazing, I thought. I've got some of Amaz-O's best tricks—right here in my own house!

I forced myself to close the kit. I'd better stop fooling around with this stuff, I thought—before anything else happens!

I'll check it all out on Saturday. In daylight, when I have plenty of time to see how it all works.

Then I'll give the kit back to Amaz-O. On Monday.

I knew I had to return the kit. It had been wrong to take it. And crazy.

If only Amaz-O hadn't been so mean to me! He used me in his act—and then he locked me in the basement! He told me to get lost. He called me a punk!

I started to get angry all over again. Amaz-O doesn't deserve to get his magic kit back, I thought.

But deep down I knew I had to return it. I wanted to do the right thing. I'd check out the tricks, then give them back.

Of course, I didn't know then how dangerous the kit was. I didn't know the trouble it would cause.

If I had known, I would have returned the case *that night*!

"Another day of work," Mum sighed at the breakfast table the next morning. "I'm absolutely dreading it. Those students just drive me crazy."

Dad grabbed a doughnut and gazed out the window. "It's raining," he said unhappily. "I probably won't sell a single car today."

Ginny and I exchanged glances. Mum and Dad had no idea we had sneaked out the night before.

I slumped into a chair and ate my cereal. I was sleepy. I'm not used to staying up so late.

"You look tired, Tim," Mum said, sitting across from me. She glanced at Ginny. "So do you, honey."

"Didn't you two get any sleep?" Dad asked.

"Sure we did," I replied.

Ginny grinned. "Not that much sleep. Tim and I have a secret!"

The little brat! I kicked her under the table.

"Ow!" she cried. "Tim kicked me!"

"Don't kick your sister," Dad scolded. "I have to leave." He picked up his briefcase and kissed Mum goodbye. "Off to another day of torture. See you tonight, kids."

Dad left. Mum started clearing away the breakfast dishes. "Did you say something about a secret?" she asked.

"No!" I insisted. "Ginny didn't say anything about a secret. She said, 'Tim and I want a wee pet.'"

Mum shot me a weird look. "A what? A wee pet?"

"Yeah," I said. "You know, a little pet. A nice little kitten or something. Ginny's learning about Scotland in school now. She's picked up some Scottish words, right, Ginny? She's been running around calling everything 'wee'."

"I have not," Ginny protested. "I've never called anything 'wee' in my life! And I'm not learning about Scotland in school!"

"Yes, you *are*," I insisted.

"What in the world are you two talking about?" Mum carried the pile of cereal bowls to the sink.

"We did a bad thing, Mum," Ginny blurted out. "Ow!" I kicked her again, but that didn't stop her.

"We sneaked out last night, Mum. We rode our bikes to Midnight Mansion to see the magic show. We didn't get back until after midnight. I'm sorry, Mum. Please don't get angry. Tim made me do it. I didn't want to."

I covered my face with my hands. Why does Ginny have to be such a big mouth?

I'm doomed, I thought. *Doomed!*

"What did you say, Ginny?" Mum asked, wiping her hands on a towel. "I was running water in the sink, and I couldn't hear you."

I let out a long breath. I couldn't believe my luck. I glared at Ginny and kicked her again—really hard this time.

"Nothing, Mum," Ginny murmured. "I didn't say anything."

"You two better get ready for school," Mum said.

I pushed my chair away from the table and dragged Ginny out of hers. "We'll be ready in a minute, Mum," I said.

"What is your problem?" I whispered to Ginny in the hall. "You could've got us in big trouble!"

"*You* would get in trouble. Not me," Ginny replied. "You're the big brother. You *made* me go."

"I didn't make you do anything. And anyway, you promised not to tell!"

"You promised not to peek into Amaz-O's kit until Saturday," Ginny reminded me. "But I sneaked up to the attic this morning—and I know you looked! You opened that bag! You even played with some of the stuff!"

"Me? I did not!" I lied.

"Yes, you did. One of the sleeves of a jacket was sticking out of the kit. And I found a scarf on the floor. You big fat liar!"

"So what? You'll still get to see the stuff on Saturday."

"You promised," Ginny repeated. She flicked my nose. "Boi-oi-oing."

I stormed into my room. There's no arguing with Ginny. She does whatever she wants—promise or no promise.

She's always getting me into trouble, I thought angrily. She drives me crazy! I wish there were some way I could pay her back. Some way to pay her back for everything.

Little did I realize I would soon find it.

"Are you sure you kids don't want to go to the antiques show with us?" Dad asked. "You might see some neat old junk there."

"We're sure," I insisted. Saturday morning had arrived, and all I could think about was Amaz-O's magic kit. I couldn't wait to get my hands on it.

I wished my parents would hurry up and leave.

"All right," Mum said, kissing Ginny and then me. "There's tuna salad in the fridge for lunch. We won't be back until dinnertime."

"Be good," Dad added.

"*I'll* be good," Ginny declared. "I don't know about *Tim*."

I tried to shove her, but she dodged me. "I'll be good," I promised. "I'm always good."

Mum rolled her eyes. "Just don't fight too much," she said. "'Bye."

Ah. At last. As soon as they were gone, I raced to the phone and rang Foz's number.

"The coast is clear," I told him. "Come on over."

I'd told Foz all about the show at Midnight Mansion and Amaz-O's magic kit. He begged me to let him see the cool tricks in Amaz-O's bag.

As soon as Foz arrived, we all trooped up to the attic. Ginny made a beeline for the magic kit. I blocked her.

"Heee-ya!" She leaped into a pre-karate chop stance. "Out of my way!"

"Ginny—wait!" I pleaded. "There's a lot of weird stuff in that bag. Let me show it to you my way."

"Okay." She relaxed. "But don't forget you're supposed to share it with me."

I pulled up two chairs. "You guys sit here," I said to Ginny and Foz. "And get ready for the greatest magic show in the history of the world!"

I reached into the toy chest and pulled out Amaz-O's magic kit. I held it up in front of Foz and Ginny. "First," I began in my magician voice, "gaze deeply into the magic trove."

I held the bag near their faces. They stared at it. I yanked it open.

Kaboom! It made the exploding sound, just as it did the first time I opened it.

Ginny and Foz fell off their chairs!

"What happened?" Foz moaned, clutching his head. "That thing blew up in my face!"

I cracked up. "It's only a sound effect," I explained.

"Not funny," Ginny complained.

"You should have seen your faces," I said gleefully. I reached into the black sack that held the three shells and the red ball. I set the shells in a row on a small table.

"Watch closely," I said. I held up the red ball. "See this ball? I'll place it under one of these shells." I pretended to tuck the ball under the middle shell. But secretly I palmed the ball and flicked it up my sleeve.

I began moving the shells over the table, shifting their places.

"Keep your eyes on the middle shell," I instructed. Then I stopped moving the shells.

"Which shell is the ball under?" I asked.

"That one," Ginny said, pointing to the shell on the right.

"Are you *sure*?" I prompted. "Foz, where do you think the ball is?"

"The same one as Ginny," he said. "I watched it the whole time."

"If you say so," I said. I was sure the ball wasn't under that shell—it wasn't under any of them. I felt the ball rubbing against my wrist.

I lifted the shell—and gasped. There *was* a ball under there. A red ball, just like the one I'd palmed.

"I was right!" Ginny crowed. "That's a stupid trick."

"But this is impossible!" I cried. I let the first ball fall out of my sleeve. I *had* palmed it.

"This is very strange," I muttered. "Let me try again."

I dropped the first ball on the floor. I picked up the second ball and pretended to slip it under a different shell. I palmed the ball and tucked it up my sleeve again.

"Here we go," I said, shifting the shells all over the table. I slid the shells around a little longer, then stopped.

"The ball is under the first shell," Foz said.

"Yes, the first shell," Ginny agreed.

"This time you're wrong!" I cried. I lifted the first shell. Another red ball!

Ginny sneered. "You're a real ace, Tim."

"Wait a second," I said. I lifted up the other two shells. All three of them had red balls under them!

"This isn't working at all," I grumbled. I set the shells down, then lifted them again. More balls! There were now three balls under each shell!

"This isn't the shell game I know." I was mystified. "This must be some other trick."

"It's way better than your dumb trick," Ginny said. "Those balls are coming out of nowhere!"

The shells began to dance as balls bubbled out

of them like popcorn. Ten balls. Twenty balls. Little red balls covered the table and bounced to the floor.

"They're still coming!" Foz cried in amazement. "We're going to be up to our necks in red balls!"

"How do I stop this thing?" I wondered.

Can I stop it?

21

I snatched up the shells and tossed them into their black sack. Then I grabbed all the red balls I could and stuffed them in, too.

"Help me, you guys!" I pleaded.

Ginny and Foz fell to their knees, gathering up red balls. We shoved them all into the sack. I pulled the string that closed it and dropped it into the magic kit.

The black sack kept bubbling. Red balls started bursting out of it.

"Stop that!" I yelled. I reached into the magic case and pulled out the first thing I touched. Then I snapped the case shut.

"I don't really get that trick," Ginny complained.

"Here's another trick," I said. "This one will be better." In my hand I held a flattened top hat. "Let's see what this does."

I punched the top hat open and placed it on my head.

"It's just a hat," Foz said, fidgeting. "It's kind of hot up here. Can we go down to the kitchen and get something to eat?"

"You guys don't get it," I said. "This is *Amaz-O*'s magic case! Okay, so I don't know how anything works yet. Once we figure it out, we could put on the best magic show ever! I could become a famous magician!"

"And I could be a famous magician's sister." Ginny yawned. "Big deal."

"That hat looks way cool on you," Foz said. "Now can we get something to eat?"

"I'm hungry, too," Ginny added.

"Wait!" I cried. I felt something move under the hat. I whipped it off.

"A white dove!" Foz cried.

"That's a good trick," Ginny admitted.

I shook the dove off my head. "How do you get it back in the hat?" I asked. Before I had a chance to try, another dove popped out of the hat.

I set the second dove on the floor. "There's another one!" Foz shouted.

A third dove flew out of the hat and settled on top of an old lamp. Out popped a fourth, and a fifth . . .

Foz started laughing. "These tricks are totally out of control!"

"This is no joke, Foz!" I snapped.

"We're going to be in major trouble," Ginny

warned. "We've got to find a way to get rid of these birds."

The attic was quickly filling up with flapping fluttering doves—and they kept coming. I knew we had to get rid of them—but how?

"Maybe there's something in here that will help." I ripped open the magic case. *Kaboom!* It made that stupid exploding sound again. Dozens of little red balls flew into my face.

"I'm really getting sick of this," I muttered.

I brushed away piles of balls. I pulled out a long black stick with a white tip. A magic wand!

"Maybe this will help!" I cried. I hoped it would. The attic was a total mess—white doves and red balls everywhere.

"This is the answer," I declared. "Amaz-O probably uses this wand to make the magic stop."

"I hope you're right," Ginny said. "If that doesn't work, you and I are going to have to run away from home."

"It'll work," I insisted. "It's got to."

I waved the wand in the air. "Stop!" I shouted. "Everything stop!"

Did it work?

No.

More doves flew out of the hat. More red balls bubbled out of the black sack.

"That magic wand is the only thing in there that *doesn't* work!" Foz joked.

"Be quiet!" I snapped. "I've got to think!"

"Yikes!" Ginny screamed. "A snake!"

She pointed at the magic case. A snake slithered out of it. Then a second, a third.

The mechanical snakes had come back to life!

Hissing snakes soon covered the floor, wriggling over the bouncing red balls. Dove feathers fell from the ceiling. The attic was so crowded I could hardly see across the room.

Ginny yelped as a snake began to crawl up her leg. "Let's get out of here!" she cried.

She yanked open the attic door. She and Foz hurried downstairs. I grabbed the magic case and followed them. A snake slithered after me.

"Get back in there!" I yelled. I picked up the snake and threw it into the attic room. I shut the door. I pushed on it to make sure it was closed. Then I ran downstairs and out to the back garden.

A gust of March wind slapped my face. Ginny's long hair flew out behind her.

"Snakes—yuck!" she squealed. "Tim—what are we going to do? When Mum and Dad see the attic, we're dead meat!"

Foz stared at the magic case. "What did you bring that out for? It's dangerous!"

"It's okay if we stay outside," I told him. "So what if a bunch of birds comes out? They'll fly away."

I wasn't as sure about that as I sounded. But I couldn't give Amaz-O's case back without seeing everything in it first. I just couldn't.

"Hurry up, Tim," Ginny whined. "I'm starving. It's lunchtime!"

"Wait. Wait." I opened the magic case. *Kaboom!* It didn't sound so loud outside— especially with the wind blowing as hard as it was.

I held the magic wand poised between my fingers. What does this thing do? I wondered.

I waved it around, trying out new magician names. "The Great Incredible-O. Mister Ter-rifico—that's not bad. Get out of there, Ginny!" She was rummaging through the magic kit.

"You promised we'd share it, remember?" she snapped. Then her face brightened. "Hey! Great!" She pulled a carrot out of Amaz-O's bag. "Just what I needed—something to eat."

"Put that back!" I ordered.

"It's still fresh," she said. "Yum!"

She opened her mouth, ready to bite the carrot.

"Ginny—no!" I cried. "Maybe you shouldn't eat that. Maybe—"

Ginny never listens to me.

She crunched down on the carrot.

A flash of white light blinded me for a moment.

When my eyes focused, I saw the most amazing thing I'd ever seen in my life!

The carrot dropped to the grass. Ginny's nose twitched. Then she began to shrink.

As she shrank, her hair turned from blonde to white. Her nose turned pink. White fur and whiskers sprouted from her face. She grew smaller, furrier, whiter . . .

"I don't believe it!" Foz gasped. "Your sister— she's a rabbit!"

Ginny sat on the grass, twitching her little pink nose. She stared at me with her rabbity eyes. She waved her little paws and made angry, rabbity noises.

"Man, she is *steamed*!" Foz cried.

I was stunned. "I wished it," I murmured. "And now it's come true."

"What are you talking about?" Foz demanded. He grabbed me by the shoulders. "Get it together, Tim. We've got to do something! What's going to happen when your parents get home?"

94

"I told Ginny I'd turn her into a rabbit," I explained, still dazed. "To get back at her for ruining all my magic shows. And now she *is* a rabbit!"

Ginny the rabbit rose on her hind legs, gesturing angrily at me. Then she bounced up and thumped my shin with one of her big rabbit feet.

"Ow!" I cried. "That hurts as much as one of her karate kicks!"

"Look in the kit, Tim," Foz urged me. "There's got to be some way to change her back."

"You're right. There's got to be!" My eyes fell on the carrot in the grass. "The carrot," I said. "When Ginny bit it, she turned into a rabbit. But maybe if a rabbit bites it, it turns into a girl!"

Foz shook his head. "Huh?"

I snatched up the carrot. "We've got to try it. There's nothing to lose, right? She's already a rabbit. What else could happen to her?"

I shoved the end of the carrot towards Ginny's mouth. "Come on, Ginny. Take another bite."

She stared at the carrot suspiciously. She clamped her mouth shut and turned her face away.

"You little brat!" I shouted. "You *want* me to get in trouble, don't you! You want to stay a rabbit just to get me in trouble!"

Foz grabbed the carrot out of my hand. "Calm down, Tim. You're scaring her!"

Ginny's long rabbit ears perked up—she heard something. I heard it, too. A car coming. Pulling into the driveway!

"Hurry, Ginny!" I cried. "I think Mum and Dad are home. Take a bite of the carrot. It'll turn you back into a girl. I know it will!"

Ginny eyed me suspiciously. She sniffed the carrot with her twitchy pink nose.

"Hurry!" I shouted again.

She opened her mouth and took a nibble of carrot.

Foz and I watched her in a panic. "Please let it work," I prayed. "Please let it work!"

Ginny's rabbit nose twitched. Her ears stood straight up. Then they flopped down.

Nothing happened. She was still a rabbit.

"Mum and Dad!" I cried. "They're here! Foz—stay with Ginny. If Mum and Dad ask, say she's your sister's rabbit!"

I ran to the driveway. A car was backing out—not Mum and Dad. Just somebody turning around in our driveway.

Whew. Close one.

The wind gusted as I ran back to Foz and Ginny. Foz was on his knees, digging through the magic kit. Ginny hopped up and down impatiently.

The magic wand lay in the grass. Maybe this will work now, I hoped, picking it up. I've got to change her back!

I waved the wand over Ginny. "Turn my sister back into a girl!" I cried.

Nothing.

"Maybe you need to say the spell in a rhyme," Foz suggested. "Magicians always do that."

"Okay." I waved the wand again. "Let me think . . . Magic wand, winds that whirl, turn Ginny back into a girl!"

The wand began to shake. "Something's happening!" I shouted.

The white tip of the wand broke open. Out popped a white silk handkerchief.

"Wow!" Foz gasped. A blue one flew out, then a red one, then a yellow one. The wind blew them away before I could catch them.

I turned back to Ginny. Still a rabbit.

"It didn't work," I said unhappily. I tossed the wand into the grass. "It only makes stupid handkerchiefs."

I crossed over to the magic case. Ginny leaped at me, trying to bite my leg.

"Watch out!" I warned her. "I'm trying to help you!"

She twitched her nose in disgust.

Foz moved aside as I dived into the magic kit. I dumped everything out. A slip of paper tumbled out of a pocket in the case.

I snatched it up. At the top of the paper I saw the word INSTRUCTIONS.

"Look!" I cried. "Instructions!" I patted Ginny between the ears. 'I'll have you back to normal in a second."

I raised the paper to read what it said.

"'Instructions. To use the magic top hat . . .' No. That's not what I need right now . . ."

"Hurry, Tim!" Foz said.

I scanned the paper, searching for anything about rabbits. "Here's something!" I announced. "'The magic carrot . . .'"

Just then a strong gust of wind blasted across the garden. The paper flew out of my hands.

"No!" I shouted, grasping for the paper. "I need that!" I watched helplessly as it flew out of my reach—high up into the sky.

"Get that paper!" I screamed. The wind blew it across the garden. I darted after it.

Foz zoomed ahead of me, yelling, "I've got it! I've got it!" The paper floated within his reach. He dived for it.

Whoosh! Another strong gust of wind. The paper fluttered away. Foz fell flat on his face.

I ran past him, following the paper. It blew across my neighbour's garden.

"Get it!" Foz shouted, racing after me. "It's headed for the woods!"

The wind died for a minute. The paper settled on the grass.

I pounced on it. But the wind picked up before I landed. The paper blew away again.

"Rats!" I cried.

"There it goes!" Foz shouted. The paper drifted towards the stream.

The paper floated above the stream, then

landed in the water. Foz zipped across the garden to grab it.

"Don't let it get wet!" I screamed.

Too late. The paper was soaked.

"I've got it!" Foz shouted. He leaned over the stream and snatched at the paper. But the current carried it away.

Foz and I chased it down the stream, panting. But we couldn't run as fast as the current.

"It's getting away," I huffed. A few seconds later we lost sight of it.

Foz and I collapsed on the ground.

"That's it," I groaned. "We'll never get it back now. So how do I turn Ginny back into a girl?"

Foz heaved himself to his feet and pulled me up by the hand. "Don't panic, Tim. Panicking isn't going to help."

Great advice.

We hurried back to Ginny. I hoped maybe she'd magically turned back into a girl while we were gone. No such luck.

Ginny knew we hadn't found the instructions. She bounced around the garden, squealing angry rabbit squeals.

Foz rubbed his short hair as he watched her. "Boy, she's really stressed," he said.

I fell to my knees to talk to her. "Don't worry, Ginny," I soothed. "I've got an idea. I'm going to take you to Amaz-O right now. He'll turn you back into a girl. I'm sure he will."

With one of her long rabbit ears, Ginny flicked my nose. She couldn't say "Boi-oi-oing." She didn't have to. I knew what she meant.

"Let's pick this stuff up," I said to Foz. We began to gather all the tricks off the grass and pile them into Amaz-O's magic case. "Amaz-O won't want to help us if I don't give him back his magic kit."

Foz took my bike, balancing the magic kit on the handlebars. I picked up Ginny. "Come on, little rabbit sister," I cooed. She let me pull her up by the back—then nipped me on the wrist!

"Ow!" I dropped her. "Do you want me to help you or not?"

She hopped up and down angrily. I knew what she was thinking. If I didn't change her back into a girl, I'd be in as much trouble as she was. I had no choice.

I reached for her again. "Don't bite me this time," I warned her. "Or I'll put a muzzle over that little snout of yours."

She squirmed in my arms but didn't bite. I set her in the basket on her bike.

"To Midnight Mansion," I told Foz. We set off, pedalling hard against the strong wind.

I rode through town in a daze. Ginny's long white ears waved in my face.

Amaz-O's words rang in my ears. "Beat it, punk!" he'd said. I wondered if he'd really help me.

He's got to, I told myself. He'll be glad to get his magic kit back.

I'll make him help, I decided. I won't give him the kit until he turns Ginny back into a girl.

We pulled into the car park in front of Midnight Mansion. The old castle looked just as scary in the daytime as it did at night. There were no floodlights casting shadows on the stone towers. But the grey, vine-covered walls gave the place a spooky, abandoned feeling.

I skidded to a stop in front of the mansion. Foz carried the magic kit. I grabbed Ginny out of the bike basket.

"Behave," I warned her as we climbed the front steps to the mansion. "Remember, I'm trying to help you. Don't go biting me or anything."

She twitched her nose at me. She lifted her little rabbit lips and bared her tiny rabbit teeth.

"Go ahead—bite me," I whispered. "See how you like spending the rest of your life as a rabbit. You don't even *like* lettuce!"

She closed her mouth and twitched her nose again. It doesn't matter whether she's a girl or a rabbit, I thought. Either way she's a pain in the neck.

We stopped at the top of the steps.

"Oh, no!" I gasped. "I don't believe it!"

The sign on the front door read SORRY, WE'RE CLOSED.

"No!" I cried. I banged my forehead against the door.

Foz said, "This place gives me the creeps. It looks like Count Dracula's castle." He shivered. "Let's get out of here."

He set the magic case down. "Amaz-O's magic kit is so heavy. Do you think we can leave it by the door?"

I glared at him. "*No*, we can't leave it by the door. And we're not going home. Not yet."

I squeezed Ginny in my arms, thinking. "Okay, so the place is closed. But Amaz-O could be in there, rehearsing or something. Right?"

"He could be, I guess," Foz said. "But chances are—"

"We've got to take that chance," I insisted. I tried the front door. Locked. Of course.

"There must be another way in," I said. "A back door or something." I dashed down the steps and around the side of the club.

"Bring the case, Foz!" I ordered.

He followed me, lugging the kit. I kept my eyes peeled for guards.

At the back of the mansion we found a door. I tried it. It opened easily!

We crept inside. We found ourselves in the club's kitchen. It was long, narrow, and shiny clean. The lights were off, but we could see by the light from a window at one end.

Foz paused in front of a huge, stainless steel refrigerator. "I'll bet they've got some great food in here," he whispered. "Lemon meringue pie or something."

I tugged at his arm. "This is no time for a snack!" I snapped. "Come on!"

We left the kitchen and entered a long, dark hallway. I recognized that hall. It was the same hallway I'd walked down after my escape from the basement—the *first* time Amaz-O let me down.

"There'd better not be a second time," I muttered under my breath.

We tiptoed down the dark hall. Up ahead I saw the door to Amaz-O's dressing room. It was half-open. A dim light spilled out into the hallway.

Yes! I thought to myself. That's a good sign.

With Ginny in my arms, I crept up to the door. Please, please let him be in there, I prayed. Please be here, Amaz-O. Please help us.

I stopped in front of the door. I took a deep breath.

"Mr Amaz-O? Are you here?"

No reply.

I tried again. "Mr Amaz-O? Hello?"

"He's not here," Foz said. "Let's go."

"Shhh!" I pushed the door open and crept into the dressing room. One small lamp cast a dim pool of light on the dressing table. The great Amaz-O sat on the couch, his left side facing the door. He was staring at the wall. He didn't seem to notice us.

"Mr Amaz-O?" I said politely. "It's me again. The kid you made disappear in your magic show."

I thought Amaz-O would turn his head to face us now, but he didn't. He didn't do anything. He just sat there.

Man, I thought. He really hates kids. Or he hates his fans. Or he hates all people. Or something.

When I become a great magician, I vowed, I won't be like Amaz-O. I won't let my fame go to my head. I'll be nice to people. This is ridiculous.

I didn't care what Amaz-O's problem was. I needed his help—badly. And I wouldn't give up until I got it.

I stepped further into the dressing room. "Mr Amaz-O, I'm sorry to bother you. But I really need your help. It's important."

Amaz-O didn't move. He stared at the wall. Silent.

"Do you think he's asleep?" Foz whispered.

I shrugged. I took another breath and crept closer to the couch.

"I know you told me to beat it," I said. "I wouldn't bother you if it wasn't a matter of life and death—I swear."

Still no response. I turned back to Foz, who cowered in the doorway. He looked as if he were ready to run for it. I waved him into the room.

Foz stepped in. He set the magic kit on the floor, shaking.

I stared at Amaz-O. He ignored me. Who does he think he is? I thought angrily. He can't treat me this way! I'm not leaving until he helps me turn Ginny back into a girl.

I steeled myself and approached the magician. He didn't look at me. I tapped him on the shoulder.

He toppled over on to his side. *Thunk!*

Foz gasped. "Is he—? Is he—?"

I peered at the body on the couch. "He isn't alive!" I cried. "Amaz-O isn't alive!"

"Oh, no!" Foz was wringing his hands in terror. "Oh, no! He's dead! He's dead! Help!"

"He's not dead," I said. "He's a dummy!

"Amaz-O is nothing but a big wooden puppet!"

How could it be possible? I stared at the puppet on the couch. I couldn't resist touching its cheek—then pinching it—just to be sure.

Oh, wow!

It was true. Amaz-O was made of wood.

Foz sputtered, "But—I saw him on TV. He looked totally real."

"And I saw him live," I said. "On stage. I stood right next to him, and he made me disappear!"

How can this be? I wondered. How can the greatest magician in the world be a puppet?

"This can't be the guy you saw," Foz insisted, poking at the dummy. "This is probably just a dummy he keeps around for fun. The real Amaz-O has got to be around here somewhere."

Rabbit Ginny squirmed angrily in my arms. "Calm down," I ordered, trying to pet her.

She growled. I've never heard of a rabbit growling before. Only a Ginny-rabbit would growl.

Amaz-O, my idol, I thought bitterly. What a fake he turned out to be. Not only was he a jerk to me—he's not even a real person! He's a puppet!

"What are we going to do?" Foz asked.

I shook my head. I had no idea. "Now I'll never get Ginny changed back into a girl," I said. "Mum and Dad are going to *murder* me."

"Why don't you tell them she ran away?" Foz suggested. "They'll never believe you turned her into a rabbit, anyway."

"Why would she run away?" I demanded. "She was their little darling. She could do no wrong. *I'm* the one who should run away."

Foz lifted the Amaz-O puppet's head, studying it. "I wonder how this thing works . . ." he said.

A low voice suddenly growled, "Hey, punk— I told you to beat it!"

I froze. "Did you say something, Foz?" I asked.

He shook his head, eyes wide. He'd heard the voice, too.

"So beat it! Get out of here!" the voice growled.

I glanced around the room. I didn't see anyone.

"Did the puppet talk?" I asked Foz.

"I—I don't think so," he stammered. "The voice came from the other side of the room."

"The puppet didn't talk, dummy," the voice grumbled. I turned to find it. I gazed across the room. Amaz-O's white rabbit sat on a chair in front of the dressing table.

"I told you to get lost. Now get lost!" the rabbit growled.

"Tim—did—did you see that?" Foz stammered. "I think that rabbit talked."

"Of course I talked, stupid," the rabbit snarled.

"You talked?" I echoed in amazement.

"I guess that thing on the couch isn't the only dummy in this room," the rabbit snapped. "I can do lots of things. I'm a magician."

Foz and I stared at the rabbit, stunned. Even Ginny stopped squirming in my arms.

"You're not a magician," Foz said. "You're a rabbit."

The rabbit's ears twisted. "Duh. You guys are really quick. You know that?"

"You don't have to be so mean," I protested.

"*You* don't have to be so stupid," the rabbit replied. "I may *look* like a rabbit. But so does your little sister. Am I right?"

"He's got a point," Foz admitted.

"I am the great Amaz-O," the rabbit announced. "In person. That dummy on the couch is a puppet I had built to look like me— the old me."

My jaw fell open. "*You're* Amaz-O? What happened to you?"

The rabbit sighed. "It's a long story. Let's just

112

say I had a rival—a real powerful one. A sorcerer, actually."

Foz gasped. "A sorcerer? Do they really exist?"

"I'm telling you about one, aren't I?" the rabbit shouted.

"Yes, but—"

"So be quiet and listen to the story," Amaz-O, the rabbit, grumbled. "If you'd stop talking you might learn something."

Amaz-O sure was a grouch.

"Anyway, long story short," Amaz-O went on. "This sorcerer guy—Frank—"

"A sorcerer named Frank?" I cut in. I didn't mean to interrupt. It just slipped out.

The rabbit glared at me. "*Yes*, a sorcerer named Frank. You got a problem with that?"

I shook my head.

"Can I finish talking now? You got any more stupid questions?"

Foz and I both shook our heads.

"This guy's named Foz—" Amaz-O gestured towards Foz "—and you want to make fun of a guy named Frank."

"I'm sorry," I said. "I didn't mean to make fun of Frank."

"He's a very powerful guy," Amaz-O said. "I'm proof of that."

The rabbit hopped out of the chair, crossed the dressing room, and sat on the couch next to the dummy.

"Here's what happened," he began. "I was at the height of my fame. I was the most brilliant magician in the world. I made appearances on all the top TV shows. I had millions of fans. Dopey little kids like you looked up to me."

"Hey!" I protested. "Stop calling us dopey."

Amaz-O ignored me. He continued, "My tricks were the most amazing anyone had ever seen. And Frank was jealous. He was a sorcerer, working alone in a basement. He could cast amazing spells—but he was kind of ugly, with a high-pitched voice. People didn't take him seriously.

"He wanted to be famous like me, but he wasn't. So he turned me into a rabbit. Very funny, right? Ha ha. Turn the magician into a rabbit. Yuk, yuk, yuk."

Foz and I exchanged baffled glances. Amaz-O was turning out to be a little weird.

"I'm not powerful enough to reverse Frank's spell," Amaz-O went on. "I'm a magician, not a sorcerer. But I refused to let him stop me. So I built that mechanical dummy over there. I made him look just like me. And I kept on doing my shows, just as before."

"So you control the puppet?" Foz asked. "You make it look as if he's the magician, performing all the tricks?"

"I just said that, didn't I?" Amaz-O snapped. "Are you hard-of-hearing, kid?"

"You're really rude, you know that, Amaz-O?" I said. I was getting sick of his put-downs. "You're the rudest person—or rabbit, or whatever—I ever met in my life!"

Amaz-O's long ears drooped. "Hey—I'm sorry," he said. "Being a rabbit gets on my nerves. But also, I can't let people get too close— you know? I don't want anyone to find out my secret. It could ruin me."

Ginny squirmed in my arms again. I'd nearly forgotten all about her. I realized I'd better hurry up and ask Amaz-O to help me change her back.

"We're in terrible trouble, Amaz-O," I said, holding Ginny towards him. "This is my sister, Ginny. She ate some of the carrot that was in your magic kit—"

"So you confess, do you? You stole my magic kit!"

"I—I only borrowed it," I stammered. "I brought it back—see? I'm sorry."

"I'll bet you are," Amaz-O snapped.

"Can you help us, Amaz-O?" I pleaded. "Please, can you help me turn Ginny back into a girl?"

Amaz-O studied Ginny with his beady rabbit eyes. I held my breath waiting for his answer.

He settled deeper into the couch and shook his head. "Sorry," he said. "There's nothing I can do for her."

"Noooo!" I moaned, sinking into a chair. "You were my last chance. I'm doomed!"

"You didn't let me finish," Amaz-O said. "There's nothing I can do for her—because the magic will wear off by itself."

"Yo! All right!" Foz exclaimed happily. He shot both fists into the air.

"But when?" I asked. "My parents are coming home soon."

"How many bites of the carrot did she eat?" Amaz-O asked.

"Two," I replied.

"How long ago?"

"About an hour ago," I answered.

"Okay," Amaz-O said. "She should turn back into a girl in half an hour. Do you feel better now?"

I nodded and sighed with relief. That was a close one, I thought. But everything is going to be okay.

"Hey—" Foz said, jumping up. "We'd better hurry up and take Ginny home—before she turns back into a girl. We don't have enough bikes to go round!"

I pushed Ginny into his arms. "Take her home, Foz," I said. "I'll be there in a few minutes." I wanted to talk to Amaz-O a little longer.

Clutching Ginny in his arms, Foz hurried out of the dressing room. "Don't stay too long," he called over his shoulder. "I don't want to be alone with Ginny when she turns back into a girl. I have a feeling she's going to be in the mood to karate-chop somebody!"

In reply, Ginny beat her hind legs against his chest.

"I'm right behind you," I promised. Foz disappeared down the dark hallway.

"Listen, Amaz-O," I said. "I'm really sorry I stole your magic bag. I know it was a terrible thing to do."

"Shove this stupid dummy aside and sit down on the couch," Amaz-O said. I moved the dummy and sat down next to Amaz-O.

"You really love magic, don't you?" he said.

My heart started pounding. This was the heart-to-heart magician talk I'd been hoping to have with Amaz-O all along!

"It's my dream to be a magician," I told him.

117

"A great magician like you. I'd do anything. Anything!"

"Well, you were great in the show the other night," Amaz-O said. "You disappeared very well, kid."

"Thanks."

Amaz-O sat quietly for a moment. He seemed to be thinking.

"Say, kid—" he said at last. "How would you like to join the act? I'm getting really tired of working with that big wooden dummy over there."

"Me?" Now my heart was really racing. "You want me to join the act?" I got so excited I jumped off the couch. Then I quickly sat down again. "Do you mean it, Amaz-O? Do you think I could?"

Amaz-O hopped over to the dressing room door. He kicked it shut.

"Why don't we give you a try . . ."

And that's how I joined Amaz-O's act. I was so excited about being a magician, I said yes without even thinking about it. I guess I should've asked a few questions first.

Don't get me wrong. I love being on stage in front of clapping, cheering audiences.

But I don't like hiding inside the black top hat. And I hate it when the Amaz-O dummy pulls me up too hard by the ears. That really hurts.

I also hate it when they forget to clean my cage. Sometimes they forget about it for days!

I guess I made a little mistake. See, when Amaz-O said he was tired of working with the big dummy, I thought he wanted me to take the dummy's place.

I didn't realize he wanted to retire—and have me take *his* place!

I'm not complaining. Amaz-O gives me plenty of juicy lettuce and all the carrots I can eat. I even have a stage name of my own now. At last. It may not be my first choice, but it's still a professional name—"Fluffy".

The best part is, I'm on stage every night in a real magic act! My dream—my all-time dream!

How many kids—er—I mean, rabbits—can say their all-time dream came true at age twelve?

I'm really lucky—don't you agree?

Goosebumps

Egg Monsters
From Mars

My sister, Brandy, asked for an egg hunt for her tenth birthday party. And Brandy always gets what she wants.

She flashes her smile, the one that makes the dimples pop up on her cheeks. And she puts on her little baby face. Opens her green eyes wide and tugs at her curly red hair. "Please? Please? Can I have an egg hunt at my party?"

No way Mum and Dad can ever say no to her.

If Brandy asked for a red, white and blue ostrich for her birthday, Dad would be out in the garage right now, painting an ostrich.

Brandy is good at getting her way. Real good. I'm her older brother, Dana Johnson. And I admit it. Even I have trouble saying no to Brandy.

I'm not little and cute like my sister. I have straight black hair that falls over my forehead. And I wear glasses. And I'm a little chubby.

"Dana, don't look so serious." That's what Mum is always telling me.

"Dana has an old soul," Grandma Evelyn always says.

I don't really know what that means. I guess she means I'm more serious than most twelve-year-olds.

Maybe that's true. I'm not really serious all the time. I'm just curious about a lot of things. I'm very interested in science. I like studying insects and plants and animals. I have an ant farm in my room. And two tarantulas.

And I have my own microscope. Last night I studied a toenail under the microscope. It was a lot more interesting than you might think.

I want to be a research scientist when I'm older. I'll have my own lab, and I'll study anything I want to.

Dad is a kind of chemist. He works for a perfume company. He mixes things together to make new smells. He calls them *fragrances*.

Before Mum met Dad, she worked in a lab. She did things with white rats.

So both of my parents are happy that I'm into science. They encourage me. But that doesn't mean they give me whatever I ask for.

If I asked Dad for a red, white and blue ostrich for my birthday, do you know what he'd say? He'd say, "Go and play with your sister's!"

Anyway, Brandy asked for an egg hunt for

her birthday. Her birthday is a week before Easter, so it wasn't a crazy idea.

We have a very large back garden. It stretches all the way back to a small, trickling creek.

The garden is filled with bushes and trees and flower beds. And there's a big old kennel, even though we don't have a dog.

Lots of good egg-hiding places.

So Brandy got her egg hunt. She invited her entire class.

You may not think that egg hunts are exciting.

But Brandy's was.

Brandy's birthday came on a warm and sunny day. Only a few small cumulus clouds high in the sky. (I study clouds.)

Mum hurried out to the back garden after breakfast, lugging a big bucket of eggs. "I'll help you hide them," I told her.

"That wouldn't be fair, Dana," Mum replied. "You're going to be in the egg hunt too— remember?"

I'd almost forgotten. Brandy usually doesn't want me hanging around when her friends come over. But today she said that I could be in the egg hunt. And so could my best friend, Anne Gravel.

Anne lives in the house next door. My mum is best friends with Anne's mum. Mrs Gravel agreed to let Mum hide eggs all over their back garden too. So it's only fair that Anne gets to join in.

Anne is tall and skinny, and has long red-brown hair. She's nearly a head taller than me. So everyone thinks she's older. But she's twelve too.

Anne is very funny. She's always cracking jokes. She makes fun of me because I'm so serious. But I don't mind. I know she's only joking.

That afternoon Anne and I stood on the driveway and watched the kids from Brandy's class arrive at the party. Brandy handed each one of them a little straw basket.

They were really excited when Brandy told them about the egg hunt. And the girls got even more excited when Brandy told them the grand prize—one of those expensive American Girl dolls.

Of course the boys started to grumble. Brandy should have had a prize a boy might like. Some of the boys started using their baskets as Frisbees. And others began wrestling in the grass.

"I was a lot more sophisticated when I was ten," I muttered to Anne.

"When you were ten, you liked Ninja Turtles," Anne replied, rolling her eyes.

"I did not!" I protested.

"Yes, you did," Anne insisted. "You wore a Ninja Turtle T-shirt to school every day."

I kicked some gravel across the driveway. "Just because I wore the shirt doesn't mean I liked them," I replied.

Anne flung back her long hair. She sneered at me. I hate it when Anne sneers at me. "You had Ninja Turtle cups and plates at your tenth birthday party, Dana. And a Ninja Turtle table-cloth. And we played some kind of Ninja Turtle Pizza Pie-throwing game."

"But that doesn't mean I liked them!" I declared.

Three more girls from Brandy's class came running across the lawn. I recognized them. They were the girls I call the Hair Sisters. They're not sisters. But they spend all their time in Brandy's room after school doing each other's hair.

Dad moved slowly across the grass towards them. He had his camcorder up to his face. The three Hair Sisters waved to the camera and yelled, "Happy Birthday, Brandy!"

Dad tapes all our birthdays and holidays and big events. He keeps the tapes on a shelf in the den. We never watch them.

The sun beamed down. The grass smelled sweet and fresh. The spring leaves on the trees were just starting to unfurl.

"Okay—everyone follow me to the back!" Brandy ordered.

The kids lined up in twos and threes, carrying their baskets. Anne and I followed behind them.

Dad walked backwards, busily taping everything.

Brandy led the way to the back garden. Mum was waiting there. "The eggs are hidden everywhere," Mum announced, sweeping her hand in the air. "Everywhere you can imagine."

"Okay, everyone!" Brandy cried. "At the count of three, the egg hunt begins! *One—*"

Anne leaned down and whispered in my ear. "Bet you five dollars I collect more eggs than you."

I smiled. Anne always knows how to make things more interesting.

"*Two—*"

"You've got a bet!" I told her.

"*Three!*" Brandy called.

The kids all cheered. The hunt for hidden eggs was on.

They all began hurrying through the back garden, bending down to pick up eggs. Some of them moved on hands and knees through the grass. Some worked in groups. Some searched through the garden on their own.

I turned and saw Anne stooping down, moving quickly along the side of the garage. She already had three eggs in her basket.

I can't let her win! I told myself. I sprang into action.

I ran past a cluster of girls around the old kennel. And I kept moving.

I wanted to find an area of my own. A place where I could grab up a bunch of eggs without having to compete with the others.

I jogged across the tall grass, making my way to the back. I was all alone, nearly to the creek, when I started my search.

I spotted an egg hidden behind a small rock. I had to move fast. I wanted to win the bet.

I bent down, picked it up, and quickly dropped it into my basket.

Then I knelt down, set my basket on the ground, and started to search for more eggs.

But I jumped up when I heard a scream.

"Aaaaaiiiiii!"

The scream rang through the air.

I turned back towards the house. One of the Hair Sisters was waving her hand wildly, calling to the other girls. I grabbed up my basket and ran towards her.

"They're not hard-boiled!" I heard her cry as I came closer. And I saw the drippy yellow yolk running down the front of her white T-shirt.

"Mum didn't have time to hard-boil them," Brandy announced. "Or to paint them. I know it's weird. But there just wasn't time."

I raised my eyes to the house. Mum and Dad had both disappeared inside.

"Be careful," Brandy warned her party guests. "If you crack them—"

She didn't finish her sentence. I heard a wet *splat*.

Then laughter.

A boy had tossed an egg against the side of the kennel.

"Cool!" one of the girls exclaimed.

Anne's big sheepdog, Stubby, came running out of the kennel. I don't know why he likes to sleep in there. He's almost as big as the kennel.

But I didn't have time to think about Stubby.

Splat.

Another egg exploded, this time against the garage wall.

More laughter. Brandy's friends thought it was really hilarious.

"Egg fight! Egg fight!" two boys started to chant.

I ducked as an egg went sailing over my head. It landed with a *craaack* on the driveway.

Eggs were flying everywhere now. I stood there and gaped in amazement.

I heard a shrill shriek. I spun around to see that two of the Hair Sisters had runny yellow yolk oozing in their hair. They were shouting and tugging at their hair and trying to pull the yellow gunk off with both hands.

Splat! Another egg hit the garage.

Craaack! Eggs bounced over the driveway.

I ducked down and searched for Anne. She's probably gone home, I figured. Anne enjoys a good laugh. But she's twelve, much too sophisticated for a babyish egg fight.

Well, when I'm wrong, I'm wrong.

"Think fast, Dana!" Anne screamed from behind me. I threw myself to the ground just in time. She heaved two eggs at once. They both whirred over my head and dropped on to the grass with a sickening *crack*.

"Stop it! Stop it!" I heard Brandy shrieking desperately. "It's my birthday! Stop it! It's my birthday!"

Thunk! Somebody hit Brandy in the chest with an egg.

Wild laughter rang out. Sticky yellow puddles covered the back lawn.

I raised my eyes to Anne. She was grinning back at me, about to let me have it again.

Time for action. I reached into my basket and pulled out the one and only egg I had picked up.

I raised it high above my head. Started to throw—but stopped.

The egg.

I lowered it and stared at it.

Stared hard at it.

Something was wrong with the egg.

Something was terribly wrong.

The egg was too big. Bigger than a normal egg. About the size of a softball.

I held it carefully, studying it. The colour wasn't right either. It wasn't egg-coloured. That creamy off-white. And it wasn't brown.

The egg was pale green. I raised it to the sunlight to make sure I was seeing correctly.

Yes. Green.

And what were those thick cracks up and down the shell?

I ran my index finger over the dark, jagged lines.

No. Not cracks. Some kind of veins. Blue-and-purple veins criss-crossing the green eggshell.

"Weird!" I muttered out loud.

Brandy's friends were shouting and shrieking. Eggs were flying all around me. An egg splattered over my trainers. The yellow yolk oozed over my laces.

But I didn't care.

I rolled the strange egg over and over slowly between my hands. I brought it close to my face and squinted hard at the blue-and-purple veins.

"Ooh." I let out a cry when I felt it pulsing.

The veins throbbed. I could feel a steady beat. *Thud. Thud. Thud.*

"Oh wow. *It's alive!*" I cried.

What had I found? It was totally weird. I couldn't wait to get it to my worktable and examine it.

But first I had to show it to Anne.

"Anne! Hey—Anne!" I called and started jogging towards her, holding the egg high in both hands.

I was staring at the egg. So I didn't see Stubby, her big sheepdog, run in front of me.

"Whooooa!"

I let out a cry as I fell over the dog.

And landed with a sickening crunch on top of my egg.

I jumped up quickly. Stubby started to lick my face. That dog has the *worst* breath!

I shoved him away and bent down to examine my egg.

"Hey!" I cried out in amazement. The egg wasn't broken. I picked it up carefully and rolled it in my hands.

Not a crack.

What a tough shell! I thought. My chest had landed on top of the egg. Pushed it into the ground. But the shell hadn't broken.

I wrapped my hands around the big egg as if soothing it.

I could feel the blue-and-purple veins pulsing.

Is something inside getting ready to hatch? I wondered. What kind of bird was inside it? Not a chicken, I knew. This was definitely not a hen's egg.

Splat!

Another egg smacked the side of the garage.

Kids were wrestling in the runny puddles of yolk on the grass. I turned in time to see a boy crack an egg over another boy's head.

"Stop it! Stop it!"

Brandy was screaming at the top of her lungs, trying to stop the egg fight before every single egg was smashed. I turned and saw Mum and Dad running across the garden.

"Hey, Anne—!" I called. I climbed to my feet, holding the weird egg carefully. Anne was frantically tossing eggs at three girls. The girls were bombarding her. Three to one—but Anne wasn't retreating.

"Anne—check this out!" I called, hurrying over to her. "You won't believe this egg!"

I stepped up beside her and held the egg out to her.

"No! Wait—!" I cried.

Too late.

Anne grabbed my egg and heaved it at the three girls.

"No—stop!" I wailed.

As I stared in horror, one of the three girls caught the egg in mid-air—and tossed it back.

I dived for it, making a head-first slide. And grabbed the egg in one hand before it hit the gravel.

Was it broken?

No.

This shell must be made of steel! I told myself. I pulled myself to my feet, gripping the egg carefully. To my surprise, it felt hot. Burning hot.

"Whoa!" I nearly dropped it.

Throb. Throb. Throb.

It pulsed rapidly. I could feel the veins beating against my fingers.

I wanted to show the egg to Mum and Dad. But they were busy breaking up the egg fight.

Dad's face was bright red. He was shouting at Brandy and pointing to the yellow stains up and down the side of the garage.

Mum was trying to calm down two girls who were crying. They had egg yolk stuck to their hair and all over their clothes. They even had it stuck to their eyebrows. I guess that's why they were crying.

Behind them Stubby was having a feast. He was running around in circles, lapping up egg after egg from the grass, his bushy tail wagging like crazy.

What a party!

I decided to take my weird egg inside. I wanted to study it later. Maybe I'd break off a tiny piece of shell and look at it under the microscope. Then I'd make a tiny hole in the shell and try to see inside.

Throb. Throb.

The veins pounded against my hand. The egg still felt hot.

It might be a turtle egg, I decided. I walked carefully to the house, cradling it in both hands.

One morning last fall, Anne had found a big box turtle on the kerb in front of her house. She carried it into her back garden and called me over. She knew I'd want to study it.

It was a pretty big turtle. About the size of a lunch box. Anne and I wondered how it got to her kerb.

Up in my room I had a book about turtles. I knew the book would help me identify it. I had hurried home to get the book. But Mum wouldn't let me go back out. I had to stay inside and have lunch.

When I got back to Anne's back garden, the turtle had vanished. I guess it wandered away.

Turtles can be pretty fast when they want to be.

As I carried my treasure into the house, I thought it might be a turtle egg. But why was it so hot? And why did it have those yucky veins all over it?

Eggs don't have veins—do they?

I hid the egg in my dressing-table drawer. I surrounded it with my balled-up socks to protect it. Then I closed the drawer slowly, carefully, and returned to the back garden.

Brandy's guests were all leaving as I stepped outside. They were covered in sticky eggs. They didn't look too happy.

Brandy didn't look too happy, either. Dad was busy shouting at her, angrily waving his arms, pointing to the gloppy egg stains all over the lawn.

"Why did you let this happen?" he screamed at her. "Why didn't you stop it?"

"I tried!" Brandy wailed. "I tried to stop it!"

"We'll have to have the garage painted," Mum murmured, shaking her head. "How will we ever mow the lawn?"

"This was the worst party I ever had!" Brandy cried. She bent down and pulled chunks of eggshell from her trainer laces. Then she glared up at Mum. "It's all *your* fault!"

"Huh?" Mum gasped. "My fault?"

"You didn't hard-boil the eggs," Brandy accused. "So it's all your fault."

Mum started to protest—but bit her lip instead.

Brandy stood up and tossed the bits of eggshell to the ground. She flashed Mum her best dimpled smile. "Next year for my birthday, can we have a Make Your Own Ice-Cream Sundae party?"

That evening I wanted to study my weird green egg. But we had to visit Grandma Evelyn and Grandpa Harry and take them out to dinner. They always make a big fuss about Brandy's birthday.

First, Brandy had to open her presents. Grandma Evelyn bought her a pair of pink fuzzy slippers that Brandy will never wear. She'll probably give them to Stubby as chew toys.

Brandy opened the biggest box next. She pulled out a pair of pink-and-white pyjamas. Brandy made a big fuss about them and said she really needed pyjamas. She did a pretty good acting job.

But how excited can you get over pyjamas?

Her last present was a twenty-five-dollar gift certificate for the CD store at the mall. Nice present. 'I'll go with you to make sure you don't pick out anything lame," I offered.

Brandy pretended she didn't hear me.

She gave our grandparents big hugs. Brandy is a big hugger. Then we all went out for dinner at the new Italian restaurant on the corner.

What did we talk about at dinner? Brandy's wild birthday party. When we told Grandma and Grandpa about the egg fight, they laughed and laughed.

It wasn't so funny in the afternoon. But a few hours later at dinner, we all had to admit it was pretty funny. Even Dad managed a smile or two.

I kept thinking about the egg in my dressing-table drawer. When we got back home, would I find a baby turtle on my socks?

Dinner stretched on and on. Grandpa Harry told all of his funny golfing stories. He tells them every time we visit. We always laugh anyway.

We didn't return home till really late. Brandy fell asleep in the car. And I could barely keep my eyes open.

I slunk up to my room and changed into pyjamas. Then, with a loud yawn, I turned off the light. I knew I'd fall asleep the moment my head hit the pillow.

I fluffed my pillow the way I liked it. Then I slid into bed and pulled the quilt up to my chin.

I started to settle my head on the pillow when I heard the sound.

Thump. Thump. Thump.

Steady like a heartbeat. Only louder.

Much louder.

THUMP. THUMP. THUMP.

So loud, I could hear the dressing-table drawers rattling.

I sat straight up. Wide awake now. I stared through the darkness to my dressing-table.

THUMP. THUMP. THUMP.

I turned and lowered my feet to the floor.

Should I open the drawer?

I sat in the darkness, trembling with excitement. With fear.

Listening to the steady thud.

Should I open the drawer and check it out?

Or should I run as far away as I could?

Thump, thump, THUMP.

I had to see what was happening in my dressing-table drawer.

Had the egg hatched? Was the turtle bumping up against the sides of the drawer, trying to climb out?

Was it a turtle?

Or was it something weird?

Suddenly I felt very afraid of it.

I took a deep breath and rose to my feet. My legs felt rubbery and weak as I made my way across the room. My mouth was suddenly as dry as cotton.

Thump, THUMP, thump.

I clicked on the light. Blinked several times, struggling to force my eyes to focus.

The steady thuds grew louder as I approached the dressing-table.

Heartbeats, I told myself.

Heartbeats of the creature inside the egg.

I grabbed the drawer handles with both hands. Took another deep breath.

Dana, this is your last chance to run away, I warned myself.

This is your last chance to leave the drawer safely closed.

Thump, thump, thump, thump, thump.

I tugged open the drawer and peered inside.

I stared in, amazed that nothing had changed. The egg sat exactly where I had left it. The blue-and-purple veins along the shell pulsed as before.

Feeling a little calmer, I picked it up.

"Ouch!"

I nearly dropped it. The shell was burning hot.

I cupped it in my hands and blew on it. "This is so totally weird," I murmured to myself.

Mum and Dad have to see it, I decided. Right now. Maybe they can tell me what it is.

They were still awake. I could hear them talking in their room down the hall.

I carried the egg carefully, cradling it in both hands. I had to knock on their door with my elbow. "It's me," I said.

"Dana, what is it?" Dad demanded grumpily. "It's been a long day. We're all very tired."

I pushed open their door a crack. "I have an egg I want to show you," I started.

"No eggs!" they both cried at once.

"Haven't we seen enough eggs for one day?" Mum griped.

"It's a very strange egg," I insisted. "I can't identify it. I think—"

"Good night, Dana," Dad interrupted.

"Please don't ever mention eggs again," Mum added. "Promise?"

"Well, I . . ." I stared down at the pulsing green egg in my hand. "It'll only take a second. If you'll just—"

"Dana!" Dad yelled. "Why don't you go sit on it and hatch it?"

"Clark—don't talk to Dana that way!" Mum scolded.

"He's twelve years old. He can take a joke," Dad protested.

They started arguing about how Dad should talk to me.

I muttered good night and started back to my room.

I mean, I can take a hint.

Thump. Thump. The egg pulsed in my hand.

I had a sudden impulse to crack it open and see what was inside. But of course I would never do that.

I stopped outside Brandy's room. I was desperate to show my weird treasure to somebody. I knocked on her door.

No answer.

I knocked again, a little harder. Brandy is a very heavy sleeper.

Still no answer.

I started to knock a third time—and the door flew open. Brandy greeted me with an open-mouthed yawn. "What's wrong? Why'd you wake me?"

"I want to show you this egg," I told her.

She narrowed her eyes at me. "You're serious? After what happened at my party? After the worst birthday party in the history of America, you really want to show me an egg?"

I held it up. "Yeah. Here it is."

She slammed the door in my face.

"You mean you don't want to see it?" I called in.

No reply.

Once again, I could take a hint. I carried the egg back to my room and set it down carefully in the dressing-table drawer. Then I closed the drawer and climbed back into bed.

Thump. Thump. Thump.

I fell asleep to the steady throbbing.

The next morning, I woke up just in time to watch the egg hatch.

A loud cracking sound woke me up.

Blinking, I pulled myself up on one elbow. Still half-asleep, I thought I heard Brandy cracking her knuckles.

That's one of Brandy's secret talents. She never does it when adults are around. But when you're alone, she can crack out entire symphonies on her knuckles.

Another loud crack snapped me alert.

The dressing-table. The noises were coming from my dressing-table.

I heard a long *rip*, like Velcro ripping open. Then more cracks. Like cracking bones.

And I knew it had to be the egg.

My heart started to pound. I leaped up. Grabbed my glasses and slapped them on to my face. My legs got tangled in the bedsheet, and I nearly went sprawling over the floor.

I hurtled across the room. The egg was hatching—and I had to be there in time to watch.

147

I grabbed the drawer handles and eagerly pulled the drawer open. I was so eager, I nearly pulled the drawer out of the table!

Catching my balance, I gripped the table top with both hands and stared down at the egg.

Craaaaack.

The blue-and-purple veins throbbed. A long, jagged crack split across the green shell.

Unh unh.

I heard a low grunt from inside the egg. The grunt of a creature working hard to push out.

Unnnnnh.

What a struggle!

It doesn't sound like a turtle, I told myself. Is it some kind of exotic bird? Like a parrot? Or a flamingo maybe?

How would a flamingo egg get in my back garden?

How would *any* weird egg get in my back garden?

Unnnh unnnnh.

Craaaaaack.

The sounds were really gross.

I rubbed my eyes and squinted down at the egg. It was bouncing and bobbing in the drawer now. Each grunt made the egg move.

The veins throbbed. Another crack split along the front of the shell. And thick yellow goo poured out into the drawer, seeping on to my socks.

"Yuck!" I cried.

The egg shook. Another crack. More of the thick liquid oozed down the egg and on to my socks.

The egg bobbed and bounced. I heard more hard grunting. *Unnnnh. Unnnnh.* The egg trembled with each grunt.

Yellow slime oozed as the cracks in the shell grew wider. The veins pulsed. The egg shook.

And then a large triangle of shell broke off. It fell into the drawer.

I leaned closer to stare into the hole in the egg. I couldn't really see what was inside. I could see only wet yellow blobby stuff.

Unnh-unnnnh.

Another grunt—and the eggshell crackled and fell apart. Yellow liquid spilled into the drawer, soaking my socks.

I held my breath as a weird creature pushed itself out of the breaking shell. A yellow, lumpy thing.

A baby chicken?

No way.

I couldn't see a head. Or wings. Or feet.

I gripped the dressing-table top and stared down at it. The strange animal pushed away the last section of shell. This was amazing!

It rolled wetly over my socks.

A blob. A sticky, shiny yellow blob.

It looked like a pile of very runny scrambled eggs.

Except it had tiny green veins criss-crossing all over it.

My chest felt about to explode. I finally remembered to breathe. I let out my breath in a long whoosh. My heart was thudding.

The yellow blob throbbed. It made sick, wet sucking sounds.

It turned slowly. And I saw round black eyes near its top.

No head. No face. Just two tiny black eyes on top of the lumpy yellow body.

"You're not a chicken," I murmured out loud. My voice came out in a choked whisper. "You're definitely not a chicken."

But what was it?

"Hey—Mum! Dad!" I shouted.

They had to see this creature. They had to see the scientific discovery of the century!

'Mum! Dad! Hurry!"

No response.

The lumpy creature stared up at me. Throbbing. Its tiny green veins pulsing. Its eggy body bouncing.

"Mum? Dad?"

Silence.

I stared into my drawer.

What should I do?

I had to show it to Mum and Dad. I carefully closed the drawer so it couldn't bounce out and escape. Then I went running downstairs, shouting at the top of my voice.

My pyjama trousers were twisted, and I nearly fell down the stairs. "Mum! Dad! Where *are* you?"

The house was silent. The vacuum cleaner had been pulled out of the closet. But no one was around to use it.

I burst into the kitchen. Were they still having breakfast?

"Mum? Dad? Brandy?"

No one there.

Sunlight streamed in through the kitchen window. The breakfast dishes—three cereal bowls and two coffee cups—were stacked beside the sink.

Where did they go? I wondered, my heart pounding. How could they leave when I had the

151

most amazing thing in the history of the known universe to show them?

I turned to leave the kitchen when I saw the note on the refrigerator. It was written in blue ink in Mum's handwriting. I snatched it off the magnet and read it:

"Dad and I taking Brandy to her piano lesson. Get yourself some cereal. Love, M."

Cereal?

Cereal?

How could I think about cereal at a time like this?

What should I do now?

I leaned my forehead against the cool refrigerator, struggling to think. I couldn't leave the throbbing egg blob locked up in the drawer all morning. Maybe it needed fresh air. Maybe it needed exercise. Maybe it needed food.

Food? I swallowed hard. What would it eat? What *could* it eat? It was just a lump of scrambled eggs with eyes.

I've got to take it out of there, I decided. I've got to show it to someone.

I thought instantly of Anne.

"Yes!" I exclaimed to myself. I'll take it next door and show it to Anne. She has a dog. She's really good with pets and animals. Maybe she'll have some idea of what I should do with it.

I hurried back upstairs and pulled on the jeans and T-shirt I had tossed on the floor the night before. Then I made my way to the dressing-table and slid open the drawer.

"Yuck!"

The egg blob sat in its own yellow slime. Its whole body throbbed. The tiny, round eyes stared up at me.

"I'm taking you to Anne's," I told it. "Maybe the two of us can figure out what you are."

Only one problem.

How do I take it there?

I rubbed my chin, staring down at it. Do I carry it on a plate? No. It might tumble off.

A bowl?

No. A jar?

No. It couldn't breathe.

A box.

Yes. I'll put it in a box, I decided. I opened my wardrobe, dropped to my hands and knees, and shuffled through all the junk piled on the floor.

That's how I clean my room. I toss everything into the wardrobe and shut the door. I have the cleanest room in the house. No problem.

The only problem is finding things in my wardrobe. If I'm searching for something to wear, sometimes it takes a few days.

Today I got lucky. I found what I was looking for straight away. It was a shoe box. The box my new trainers came in.

I picked up the shoe box from the clutter and climbed to my feet. Then I kicked a bunch of stuff back into the wardrobe so I could get the door closed.

"Okay!" I cried happily. I returned to the throbbing egg glob. "I'm carrying you to Anne's in this box. Ready?"

I didn't expect it to answer. And it didn't.

I pulled off the shoe box lid and set it on the top of the dressing-table. Then I lowered the box to the drawer.

"Now what?" I asked myself out loud.

How do I get it in the box? Do I just pick it up?

Pick it up in my hand?

I held the box in my left hand and started to reach into the drawer with my right. But then I jerked my hand away.

Will it bite me? I wondered.

How can it? It doesn't have a mouth.

Will it sting me? Will it hurt me somehow?

My throat tightened. My hand started to tremble. It was so gross—so wet and eggy.

Pick it up, Dana, I told myself. Stop being such a wimp. You're a scientist—remember? You have to be bold. You have to be daring.

That's true, I knew. Scientists can't back away from something just because it's yucky and gross.

I took a deep breath.

I counted to three.

Then I reached for it.

As my hand moved towards it, the creature began to tremble. It shook like a glob of yellow jelly.

I pulled back once again.

I can't do it, I decided. I can't pick it up with my bare hands. It might be too dangerous.

I watched it shake and throb. Wet bubbles formed on its eggy skin.

Is it scared of me? I wondered. Or is it trying to warn me away?

I had to find something to pick it up with. I turned and glanced around the room. My eyes landed on my baseball glove tucked on the top shelf of my bookcase.

Maybe I could pick up the egg creature in the glove and drop it into the shoe box. I was halfway across the room when I decided I didn't want to get my glove all wet and gloppy.

I need to shovel it into the box, I thought.

A little shovel would make the job easy. I walked back to the dressing-table. The egg creature was still shaking like crazy. I closed the drawer. Maybe the darkness will calm it down, I thought.

I made my way down to the basement. Mum and Dad keep all their gardening supplies down there. I found a small metal trowel and carried it back up to my room.

When I pulled open the drawer, the eggy blob was still shaking. "Don't worry, fella," I told it. "I'm a scientist. I'll be really gentle."

I don't think it understands English. As I lowered the trowel into the drawer, the green veins on the throbbing body began to pulse.

The creature started bobbing up and down. The little black eyes bulged up at me. I had the feeling the little guy was about to explode or something.

"Easy. Easy," I whispered.

I lowered the trowel carefully beside it. Then I slowly, slowly slid it under the throbbing creature.

"There. Gotcha," I said softly.

It wiggled and shook on the blade of the trowel. I began to lift it carefully from the drawer.

The shoe box sat on top of the dressing-table. I had the trowel in my right hand. I reached for the shoe box with my left.

Up, up. Slowly. Very slowly, I raised the egg creature towards the box.

Up. Up.

Almost to the box.

And the creature *growled* at me!

A low, gruff growl—like an angry dog.

"Ohhh!" I uttered a startled cry—and the trowel dropped from my hand.

"Yaaiii!" I let out another cry as it clanged across the floor—and the egg creature plopped wetly on to my trainer.

"No!"

Without thinking, I bent down and grabbed it up in my hand.

I'm holding it! I realized, my heart pounding.

I'm holding it.

What's going to happen to me?

Nothing happened.

No shock jolted my body. No rash spread instantly over my skin. My hand didn't fall off.

The creature felt warm and soft, like runny scrambled eggs.

I realized I was squeezing it tightly. Too tightly? I loosened my grip.

And lowered it into the shoe box. And fastened the lid over the top.

I set the shoe box down on the top of the dressing-table and examined my hand. It felt wet and sticky. But the skin hadn't turned yellow or peeled off or anything.

I could hear the creature pulsing inside the box.

"Don't growl like that again," I told it. "You scared me."

I grabbed some tissues and wiped off my hand. I kept my eyes on the box. The creature was bouncing around in there.

What kind of animal is it? I wondered.

I wished Mum and Dad were home. I really, really wanted to show it to them.

I glanced at the clock radio on my bedside table. Only nine o'clock. Anne might still be sleeping. Sometimes she sleeps until noon on Saturdays. I'm not really sure why. She says it makes the day go faster. Anne is a pretty weird girl.

I lifted the box with both hands. The egg creature felt surprisingly heavy. I made sure the lid was on tight. Then I carried it down the stairs and out the back door.

It was a sunny, warm day. A soft breeze made the fresh spring leaves tremble on the trees. Two houses down Mr Simpson was already mowing his back lawn. Near the garage two robins were having a tug-of-war over a fat brown earthworm.

I carried the box to Anne's back door. The door was open. I peered through the screen.

"Hi, Dana. Come in," Anne's mother called from in front of the sink.

Balancing the box against my chest, I pulled open the screen door and stepped into the kitchen. Anne sat at the breakfast table. She wore a big blue T-shirt over black bike shorts. Her red-brown hair was tied behind her head in a long ponytail.

Three guesses what she was eating for breakfast.

You got it. Scrambled eggs.

"Yo, Dana!" she greeted me. "What's up?"

"Well—"

Mrs Gravel moved to the stove. "Dana, have you had breakfast? Can I make you some scrambled eggs?"

My stomach did a flip-flop. I swallowed hard. "No. I don't think so."

"Nice fresh eggs," Mrs Gravel insisted. "I could make them fried if you don't like scrambled."

"No thanks," I replied weakly.

I felt the eggy blob bounce inside the box.

"I might need some more," Anne told her mum, shovelling in a big glob. "These eggs are great, Mum."

Mrs Gravel cracked an egg on the side of the frying-pan. "Maybe I'll make one for myself," she said.

All this egg talk was making me sick.

Anne finished her orange juice. "Hey—what's in the box? New trainers?"

"Uh . . . no," I replied. "Check this out, Anne. You won't believe what I found."

I was so eager to show it to her! Holding the box in front of me with both hands, I started across the kitchen.

And tripped over Stubby.

Again!

160

That big dumb sheepdog always got underfoot.

"Whooooaaa!" I let out a cry as I fell over the dog—and watched the shoe box fly into the air.

I landed on top of Stubby. Got a mouthful of fur.

Struggled frantically to my feet.

And saw the egg creature sail out of the box and drop on to Anne's breakfast plate.

Anne's mouth dropped open. Her face twisted in disgust. "Oh, yuck!" she wailed. "Rotten eggs! Gross! Rotten eggs!"

"No—it's alive!" I protested.

But I don't think anyone heard me. Stubby jumped up on me as I started to explain, and nearly knocked me down again.

"Down, boy! Down!" Mrs Gravel scolded. "You know better than that."

"Get this away!" Anne demanded, shoving her plate across the table.

Her mum examined the plate, then glared at me. "Dana, what's wrong with you? This isn't funny. You ruined perfectly good scrambled eggs."

"You spoiled my breakfast!" Anne cried angrily.

"No, wait—" I protested.

But I wasn't fast enough.

Mrs Gravel grabbed up the plate. She carried

it to the sink, clicked on the garbage disposal—
and started to empty the egg creature into the
roaring drain.

"Nooooo!"

I let out a shriek—and dived for the sink.

I made a wild grab and pulled the creature from the drain.

No. I pulled a handful of *scrambled eggs* from the drain!

The egg creature rolled around the sink and started to slide towards the gurgling drain. I tossed the scrambled eggs down and grabbed the creature as it started to drop towards the grinding blades.

The lumpy yellow blob felt hot in my hands. I could feel the veins throbbing. The whole creature pulsed rapidly, like a racing heart.

I raised it up to my face and examined it. Still in one piece. "I saved your life!" I told it. "Whew! What a close one!"

I balanced it carefully in my palm. It shuddered and throbbed. Wet bubbles rolled down its lumpy sides. The black eyes stared up at me.

"What *is* that thing?" Anne demanded, getting up from the breakfast table. She straightened her long ponytail. "Is it a puppet? Did you make it out of an old sock or something?"

Before I could answer, Mrs Gravel gave me a gentle push towards the kitchen door. "Get it out of here, Dana," she ordered. "It's disgusting." She pointed down. "Look. It's dripping some kind of eggy goo all over my kitchen floor."

"I—I found it out the back," I started. "I don't really know what it is, but—"

"Out," Anne's mum insisted. She held open the screen door for me. "Out. I mean it. I don't want to have to wash the whole floor."

I didn't have a choice. I carried the egg creature out into the back garden. It seemed a little calmer. At least it wasn't trembling and pulsing so hard.

Anne followed me to the driveway. The bright sun made the egg creature gleam. My hands felt slimy and wet. I didn't want to squeeze it too tightly. But I also didn't want to let it fall.

"Is it a puppet?" Anne demanded. She bent down to see it better. "Yuck. It's alive?"

I nodded. "I don't know what it is. But it's definitely alive. I found it yesterday. At Brandy's party."

Anne continued to study the yellow blob. "You found it? Where?"

"I found an egg back by the creek," I told her. "A very weird-looking egg. I took it home, and it hatched this morning. And this is what came out."

"But what *is* it?" Anne asked. She gingerly poked its side with an index finger. "Oh, yuck. It's wet and mushy."

"It's not a chicken," I replied.

"Duhhh," Anne said, rolling her eyes. "Did you figure that out all by yourself?"

"I thought it might be a turtle egg," I said, ignoring her sarcasm.

She squinted harder at it. "Do you think it's a turtle without its shell? Do turtles hatch without their shells?"

"I don't think so," I replied.

"Maybe it's some kind of mistake," Anne suggested. "A freak of nature. You know. Like you!" She laughed.

Anne has a great sense of humour.

She poked the egg creature again. The creature let out a soft wheeze of air. "Maybe you discovered a new species," Anne suggested. "A whole new kind of animal that's never been seen before."

"Maybe," I replied. That was an exciting idea.

"They'll name it after you," Anne teased. "They'll call it the Dodo!" She laughed again.

"You're not being very helpful," I said sharply. And then I had an idea.

"Know what I'm going to do with it?" I said, cupping it carefully between my hands. "I'm going to take it to that little science lab."

She narrowed her eyes at me. "What science lab?"

"You know that little lab," I replied impatiently. "The one on Denver Street. Just three blocks from here."

"I don't hang out at weird little science labs," Anne said.

"Well, I don't either," I told her. "But I've passed by that lab a million times, riding my bike to school. I'm going to take this thing there. Someone will tell me what it is."

"I'm not going with you," Anne said, crossing her skinny arms in front of her chest. "I have better things to do."

"I didn't invite you," I sneered.

She sneered back at me.

I think she was jealous that I'd found the mysterious creature and she hadn't.

"Please get me the shoe box," I said. "I left it in your kitchen. I'm going to ride my bike over to that lab right now."

Anne went inside and came back with the shoe box. "It's all sticky inside," she said, making a disgusted face. "Whatever that thing is, it sure sweats a lot."

"Maybe your face scared it!" I declared. My turn to laugh. I'm usually the serious one. I don't

166

make too many jokes. But that was a pretty good one.

Anne ignored it. She watched as I lowered the creature into the box. Then she raised her eyes to me. "You sure that isn't some kind of wind-up toy? This thing is all a big joke—isn't it, Dana?"

I shook my head. "No way. It's no joke. I'll stop by later and tell you what the scientists at the lab say about it."

I fitted the lid on the shoe box. Then I hurried to the garage to get my bike.

I couldn't wait to get to the science lab.

As it turned out, I should have stayed as far away from that place as possible.

But how could I know what was waiting for me there?

"Look out!"

Anne's stupid sheepdog ran in front of my bike just as I started down the driveway.

I jammed on the brakes. My bike squealed to a sharp stop—and the shoe box nearly toppled off the handlebars.

"Stubby—you moron!" I shrieked.

The dog loped off across the back garden, probably laughing to himself. I think Stubby gets a real thrill by tripping me up whenever he sees me.

I waited for my heart to stop thudding in my chest. Then I steadied the shoe box on the handlebars.

I started pedalling along the street, steering with one hand, keeping the other hand on top of the box.

"The scientists at the lab have got to know what this thing is," I told myself. "They've *got* to."

I usually speed down my street. But this morning I pedalled slowly. I stopped at each corner to make sure no cars were coming.

I tried to steer away from bumps in the street. But my street has a lot of potholes. Each time I hit a bump, I could hear the egg creature bouncing inside the box.

Just don't bounce out, I thought.

I pictured it bouncing out of the box, dropping on to the street, and being run over by a car.

I stopped to balance it better on the handlebars. Then I began pedalling slowly again.

Some kids from school were starting up a softball game on the playground on the next block. They called to me. I think they wanted me to join the game.

But I pretended I didn't hear them. I didn't have time for softball. I was on a scientific mission. I didn't look back. I kept pedalling.

As I turned the corner on to Denver, a city bus roared past. The whoosh of air from the bus nearly knocked me over.

As I steadied the bike, I saw the lid push up from the shoe box.

The egg creature was trying to escape!

I grabbed the box and tried to push down the lid. I pedalled faster. The lab was only a block away.

The creature pushed up against the lid.

I pushed back.

I didn't want to crush it. But I didn't want it to escape, either.

I could feel it bouncing inside the box. Pushing up against the lid.

I kept my hand on the lid, struggling to hold it down.

An estate car filled with kids rumbled past. One of the kids yelled something to me. I didn't really hear him. I was concentrating as hard as I could on keeping the egg creature inside the box.

I rolled through a stop sign. I didn't even see it. Luckily no cars were approaching.

The lab came into view on the next corner. It was a white shingled building. Very low. Only one storey tall. But very long. With a row of small, square windows along the front. It looked like a very long train carriage.

I bumped up the kerb and rode my bike on to the grass. Then I grabbed the shoe box with both hands and hopped off. The bike fell to the ground, both wheels spinning.

Gripping the box tightly in both hands, I ran across the front lawn, up to the white double doors in front.

I found a doorbell on the wall to the right of the doors. I pushed it. Pushed it again. Kept my finger on it.

When no one came to the door, I tried the knob. Pushed. Then pulled.

No. The door was locked.

I tried knocking. I pounded as hard as I could with my fist.

Then I rang the bell again.

Where was everyone?

I was about to start pounding again when I saw the sign over the door. A small, hand-printed black-and-white sign that sent my heart sinking. It read:

CLOSED SATURDAYS AND SUNDAYS.

I let out a long sigh and shoved the box under my arm. I was so disappointed. What was I going to do with this weird egg creature now?

Shaking my head unhappily, I turned and started back to my bike. I was halfway across the grass when I heard the front door open.

I turned to see an older man in a white lab coat. He had shiny white hair, parted in the middle and slicked down on the sides. His moustache was salt-and-pepper. He had pale blue eyes that peered out at me from his pale, wrinkly face.

His smile made his eyes crinkle up at the sides. "Can I help you?" he asked.

"Uh . . . yeah," I stammered. I raised the shoe box in front of me and started back across the grass. I could feel the egg creature bouncing around in there.

"Is that a sick bird?" the man asked, squinting

at the box. "I'm afraid I can't help you with that. This is a science lab. I'm not a vet."

"No. It's not a bird," I told him. I carried the box to the doorway. My heart was pounding. For some reason, I felt really nervous.

I guess I was excited about talking to a real scientist. I respect and admire scientists so much.

Also, I was excited about finally finding out what had hatched from that weird egg. And finding out what I should do with it.

The man smiled at me again. He had a warm, friendly smile that made me feel a little calmer. "Well, if it isn't a bird in there, what is it?" he asked softly.

"I was hoping you could tell me!" I replied. I shoved the shoe box towards him, but he didn't take it.

"It's something I found," I continued. "I mean, I found an egg. In my back garden."

"An egg? What kind of egg, son?"

"I don't know," I told him. "It was very big. And it had veins all over it. And it kind of breathed."

He stared at me. "An egg that breathed."

I nodded. "I put it in my dressing-table drawer. And then it hatched this morning. And—"

"Come in, son," the man said. "Come right in." His expression changed. His eyes flashed. He suddenly looked very interested.

He put a hand on my shoulder and guided me into the lab. I had to blink a few times and wait for my eyes to adjust to the dim light inside.

The walls were all white. I saw a desk and chairs. A low table with some science magazines on it. This was a waiting room, I decided. It was all very clean and modern-looking. A lot of chrome and glass and white leather.

The man had his eyes on the box in my hands. He rubbed his moustache with his fingers. "I'm Dr Gray," he announced. "I'm the managing lab scientist here."

I switched the box to my left hand so I could shake hands with him. "I want to be a scientist when I'm older," I blurted out. I could feel my face turning red.

"What's your name, son?" Dr Gray asked.

"Oh. Uh. Dana Johnson. I live a few blocks away. On Melrose."

"It's nice to meet you, Dana," Dr Gray said, straightening the front of his white lab coat. He moved to the front door. He closed it, locked it and bolted it.

That's weird, I thought, feeling a shiver of fear.

Why did he do that?

Then I remembered that the lab was closed on weekends. He probably bolts the doors when the place is closed.

"Follow me," Dr Gray said. He led the way

down the narrow white hallway. I followed him into a small lab. I saw a long table cluttered with all kinds of test tubes, specimen jars and electronic equipment.

"Set the box down there," he instructed, pointing to an empty spot on the table.

I set the box down. He reached in front of me to remove the lid. "You found this in your back garden?"

I nodded. "Back by the creek."

He carefully pulled the lid off the box.

"Oh my goodness!" he murmured.

The egg creature stared up at us. It quivered and bubbled against the side of the box. The bottom of the box was puddled with a sticky yellow goo.

"So you found one," Dr Gray murmured, tilting the box. The yellow blob slid to the other end.

"Found one?" I replied. "You mean you know what it is?"

"I thought I rounded them all up," Dr Gray replied, rubbing his moustache. He turned his pale blue eyes on me. "But I guess I missed one."

"What is it?" I demanded. "What kind of animal is it?"

He shrugged. He tilted the box the other way, making the egg creature slide to the other end. Then he gently poked the eggy blob in the back. "This is a young one," he said softly.

"A young *what*?" I asked impatiently.

"The eggs fell all over town," Dr Gray said,

poking the egg creature. "Like a meteor shower. Only on this town."

"Excuse me?" I cried. "They fell from the sky?" I wanted desperately to understand. But so far, nothing made sense.

Dr Gray turned to me and put a hand on my shoulder. "We believe the eggs fell all the way from Mars, Dana. There was a big storm on Mars. Two years ago. It set off something like a meteor shower. The storm sent these eggs hurtling through space."

My mouth dropped open. I gazed down at the quivering yellow blob in the shoe box. "This—this is a *Martian*?" I stammered.

Dr Gray smiled. "We think it came from Mars. We think the eggs flew through space for two years."

"But—but—" I sputtered. My heart was racing. My hands were suddenly ice cold.

Was I really staring at a creature from Mars?

Had I actually *touched* a Martian?

Then I had an even *weirder* thought: I found it. I picked it up from *my* back garden.

Did that mean it belonged to me?

Did I *own* a Martian?

Dr Gray bounced the creature—*my* creature—in the box. Its veins pulsed. Its black eyes stared back at us. "We don't know how the eggs made it through the earth's atmosphere," the scientist continued.

"You mean they should have burned up?" I asked.

He nodded. "Nearly everything burns up when it hits our atmosphere. But the eggs seem to be very tough. So tough they weren't destroyed."

The egg creature made a gurgling sound. It plopped wetly against the side of the shoe box.

Dr Gray chuckled. "This is a cute one."

"You have a lot of others?" I asked.

"Let me show you something, Dana." Holding the box in front of him, Dr Gray led the way through a large metal door. The door clanged heavily behind us.

A long, narrow hallway—the walls painted white—led past several small rooms. Dr Gray's lab coat made a starchy, scratchy sound as he walked. At the end of the hall, we stopped in front of a wide window.

"In there," Dr Gray said softly.

I stared into the window.

Then I stared harder.

Was he crazy? Was he playing some kind of joke on me?

"I—I can't see anything at all!" I cried.

"Hold on a second. I forgot something," Dr Gray said. He stepped over to the wall and flicked a light switch.

A light above our heads in the hallway flashed on. And now I could see through the window.

"Oh, wow!" I exclaimed as my eyes swept over the large room on the other side of the glass. I stared at a *crowd* of egg creatures!

Dozens of them.

Yellow, eggy blobs. All pulsing and quivering. Green veins throbbing.

The egg creatures huddled on the white tile floor. They looked like big globs of cookie dough on a baking sheet. Dozens of tiny, round black eyes stared out at us.

Unreal!

As I stared at them in amazement, I kept thinking they were like stuffed animals. But they weren't. They were alive. They breathed. They shook and bounced and bubbled.

179

"Would you like to go in?" Dr Gray asked.

He didn't wait for me to answer. He pulled out a small black control unit from his pocket. He pushed a button, and the door swung open. Then he opened the door wider and guided me inside.

"Whoa!" I uttered a cry when I felt a blast of cold air. "It's *freezing* in here!" I exclaimed.

Dr Gray smiled. "We keep it very cold. It seems to keep them more alert."

He held the shoe box in one hand. He motioned to the egg creatures with the other. "Once they hatch, the creatures don't like heat. If the temperature goes too high, they melt," he explained.

He lowered the box to the floor. "We don't want them to melt," he said. "If they melt, we can't study them."

Leaning over the box, he lifted my egg creature out gently. He placed it beside three or four other egg creatures. All of the yellow blobs began bouncing excitedly.

Dr Gray picked up the box and stood back up. He smiled down at the new arrival. "We don't want you to melt, do we?" he told it. "We want you to be nice and alert. So we keep it as cold in here as we can."

I shivered and rubbed my arms. I had goosebumps all over my skin. From the excitement? Or from the cold?

I wished I had worn something warmer than a T-shirt!

The egg creatures bobbed and bubbled. I couldn't take my eyes off them. Real creatures from Mars!

I watched them start to bounce towards us. They moved surprisingly fast. They kind of rolled, kind of inched their way forward. They left slimy, yellow trails behind them as they moved.

I wanted to ask Dr Gray a million questions. "Do they have brains?" I asked. "Are they smart? Can they communicate? Have you tried talking to them? Do they talk to each other? How can they breathe our air?"

He chuckled. "You have a good scientific mind, Dana," he said. "Let's take one question at a time. Which would you like me to answer first?"

'Well—" I started to reply. But I stopped when I realized what the egg creatures had done.

While Dr Gray and I talked, they had all moved quickly into a circle.

And now they had the two of us surrounded.

I spun around.

The egg creatures had moved behind us. They blocked the door. And now they were closing in on us, bubbling and throbbing, leaving a trail of slime as they slid forward.

What were they planning to do?

In a panic, I turned to Dr Gray. To my shock, he was grinning.

"They—they've trapped us!" I stammered.

He shook his head. "Sometimes they move like that. But don't be scared, Dana. They're harmless."

"Harmless?" I cried. My voice came out shrill and tiny. "But—but—"

"What can they do?" Dr Gray asked, placing a comforting hand on my trembling shoulder. "They're only blobs of egg. They can't bite you— can they? They don't appear to have mouths. They can't grab you. Or punch you. Or kick you. They have no hands or legs."

The egg creatures moved their circle closer. I watched them, my throat still tight, my legs shaking.

I knew that what Dr Gray was telling me was true.

But why were they doing this?

Why did they form a circle? Why were they closing in on us?

"Sometimes they form triangles," Dr Gray told me. "Sometimes rectangles or squares. It's as if they're trying out different shapes they've seen. Maybe this is a way they're trying to communicate with us."

"Maybe," I agreed softly. I wished the egg creatures would back away. They were little, wet blobs. But they were really giving me the creeps!

I shivered again. My breath steamed up in front of me.

It was so cold, my glasses started to fog!

I stared down at the egg creature I had brought. It had joined the circle. It bobbed and bounced with all the others.

Dr Gray turned and started to the door. I turned with him. I wanted to get out of that freezer as fast as I could!

"Thank you for bringing that one in," Dr Gray said. He shook his head. "I thought I had collected them all. What a surprise that I missed one." He scratched his hair. "You say you found it in your back garden?"

I nodded. "It was an egg. But then it hatched in my dressing-table drawer." My teeth chattered. I was so cold!

"Does that mean it's mine?" I asked Dr Gray. "I mean, does it belong to me?"

His smile faded. "I'm not really sure. I don't know what the law is about alien creatures from outer space." He frowned. "Maybe there *is* no law."

I glanced down at the little blob. The green veins along its side were bulging. Its whole body was throbbing like crazy.

Was it sorry to see me go?

No way. That's really dumb, I told myself.

"I guess you'll want to keep it for a while and study it," I said to Dr Gray.

He nodded. "Yes. I'm doing every kind of test I can think of."

"But can I come back and visit it?" I asked.

Dr Gray narrowed his eyes at me. "Come back? Dana, what do you mean by come back? You're not leaving."

"Excuse me?" I choked out. I knew I hadn't heard him correctly.

My whole body shook in a wild shiver. I rubbed my bare arms, trying to warm them.

"Did you say I'm not leaving?" I managed to ask.

Dr Gray locked his pale blue eyes on mine. "I'm afraid you can't leave, Dana. You must stay here."

A frightened cry escaped my throat. He wasn't serious! He couldn't be serious.

He can't keep me here, I told myself.

No way. He can't keep me here against my will. That's against the law.

"But . . . why?" I demanded weakly. "Why can't I go home?"

"You can understand—can't you?" Dr Gray replied calmly. "We don't want anyone to know about these space aliens. We don't want anyone to know that we've been invaded by Martians."

He sighed. "You don't want to throw the whole world into a panic—do you, Dana?"

"I—I—I—" I tried to answer. But I was too frightened. Too startled. Too cold.

I glared angrily at Dr Gray. "You have to let me go," I insisted in a trembling whisper.

His expression softened. "Please don't stare at me like that," he said. "I'm not a bad guy. I don't want to frighten you. And I don't want to keep you in this lab against your will. But what choice do I have? I'm a scientist, Dana. I have to do my job."

I stared back at him, my whole body shaking. I didn't know what to say. My eyes moved to the metal door. It was shut. But he hadn't bolted it.

I wondered if I could get to the door before he did.

"I have to study *you* too," Dr Gray continued. He tucked his hands into the pockets of his lab coat. "It's my job, Dana."

"Study me?" I squeaked. "Why?"

He motioned to my egg creature. "You touched it—didn't you? You handled it? You picked it up?"

I shrugged. "Well, yeah. I picked it up. So what?"

"Well, we don't know what kind of dangerous germs it gave you," he replied. "We don't know what kind of germs or bacteria or strange diseases these things carried with them from Mars."

I swallowed hard. "Huh? Diseases?"

He scratched his moustache. "I don't want to scare you. You're probably perfectly okay. You feel okay—right?"

My teeth chattered. "Yeah. I guess. Just cold."

"Well, I have to keep you here and study you. You know. Watch you carefully. Make sure that touching the egg creature didn't harm you or change you."

No way, I thought.

I don't care about strange germs from Mars. I don't care about egg diseases. I don't care about science.

All I care about is getting out of here. Getting home to my family.

You're not keeping me here, Dr Gray. You're not studying me.

Because I'm *outta* here!

Dr Gray was saying something. I guess he was still explaining why he planned to keep me prisoner in this freezing cold lab.

But I didn't listen to him. Instead, I took off.

I ran towards the big metal door.

The circle of egg creatures blocked my way. But I leaped over them easily. And kept running.

Gasping for breath, shivering, I reached the door.

I grabbed the handle. And glanced back.

Was Dr Gray chasing after me?

No. He hadn't moved.

Good! I thought. I caught him by surprise.

I'm gone!

I turned the door handle. Pulled hard.

The door didn't open.

I pulled harder.

It didn't budge.

I tried pushing it.

No go.

Dr Gray's voice rang in my ears. "The door is controlled electronically," he said calmly. "It's locked. It cannot be opened unless you have the control unit."

I didn't believe him. I tugged again. Then I pushed again.

He was telling the truth. The door was electronically sealed.

I gave up with a loud cry of protest. I spun around to face him. "How long do I have to stay here?" I demanded.

He replied in a low, icy voice. "Probably for a very long time."

"Step away from the door, Dana," Dr Gray ordered. "Try to calm down."

Calm down?

"You'll be okay," the scientist said. "I take very good care of my specimens."

Specimens?

I didn't want to calm down. And I didn't want to be a specimen.

"I'm a boy. Not a specimen," I told him angrily.

I don't think he heard me. He lifted me out of the way. Then he clicked the small remote unit in his hand. The door opened just long enough for him to slide through.

It made a loud click as it snapped shut behind him.

Locked in. I was locked in this freezer with three dozen Martians.

My heart pounded. I heard a shrill whistle in my ears. My temples throbbed with pain. My whole head felt ready to explode!

189

I'd never been so angry in my life.

I let out a cry of rage.

The egg creatures all began to chatter, I spun around in surprise. They sounded a little like chimps.

A roomful of chimps, chattering away.

Only they weren't chimps. They were monsters from Mars. And I was locked in, all alone with them.

A specimen.

'Noooo!" I let out another howl and ran to the long window.

"You can't leave me here!" I shrieked. I pounded on the glass with both fists.

I wanted to cry. I wanted to scream until my throat was raw. I'd never felt so angry and so frightened all at once.

"Let me out! Dr Gray—let me out of here! You can't keep me here!" I screamed. I banged on the window as hard as I could.

I'll pound till I break the glass, I told myself.

I'll break through. Then I'll climb out and escape.

I beat my fists frantically against the glass. "Let me *out* of here! You can't *do* this!"

The glass was thick and hard. No way I could break through.

"*Let me out!*" I uttered a final scream.

When I turned back into the room, the egg

creatures stopped chattering. They stared up at me with their black, button eyes.

They didn't quiver or bounce. They stood totally still. As if they had frozen.

I'm going to freeze! I realized. I rubbed my bare arms. But it didn't help warm me. My hands were ice cold.

Icicles are going to form on me, I thought. I'm going to freeze to death in here. I'm going to turn into a human Popsicle.

The egg creatures stood so still. Their eyes were all locked on me. As if they were studying me. As if they were trying to decide what to do about me.

Suddenly my egg creature broke the silence. I recognized it by the blue veins down its front. It started to chatter loudly.

The other egg creatures turned, as if listening to it.

Was it talking to them? Was it communicating in some weird Martian chatter language?

"I hope you're telling them all how I saved your life!" I called to it. "I hope you're telling them what a good guy I am. You almost went down the drain—remember?"

Of course the egg creature couldn't understand me.

I don't know why I was shouting at it like that. I guess I was totally losing it. Totally freaked.

As the egg creature chattered on, I stared at

the others. They all listened in silence. I started to count them. There were so many of them—and so *few* of me!

Were they friendly? Did they like strangers? Did they like humans?

How did *they* feel about being locked up in this freezing cold room?

Did they feel anything at all?

These were questions I didn't really want to know the answers to.

I just wanted to get out of there.

I decided to try the window again. But before I could move, my egg creature stopped talking.

And the others started to move.

Silently, they huddled together. Pressed together into a wide yellow wedge.

And rolling faster than I could imagine, they attacked.

"Hey—!" I uttered a startled cry and backed up.

The wedge of egg creatures rolled forward. Their bodies slapped the floor wetly as they bounced towards me.

I retreated until my back hit the window.

Nowhere to run.

"What do you want?" I screamed. My voice came out high and tight in panic. "What are you going to do?"

I turned and banged on the window again, pounding with open hands. "Dr Gray! Dr Gray! Help me!"

Did they plan to roll over me? To swallow me up?

To my surprise, the egg creatures stopped a few inches in front of me. They twirled and bounced until they had formed a circle once again.

Then, moving quickly and silently, they shifted back into a big yellow triangle.

I stared down at them, shivering, my teeth chattering.

They're not attacking, I decided.

But what *are* they doing?

Why are they forming these shapes? Are they trying to *talk* to me?

I took a deep breath, trying to calm my panic.

You're a scientist, Dana, I reminded myself. Act like a scientist. Not a frightened kid. Try to talk back to them.

I thought hard for a few seconds. Then I raised my hands in front of me. And I formed a circle with my pointer fingers and thumbs.

I held the circle up so the egg creatures could all see it. And waited to see if they did anything.

The yellow blobs had formed a wide triangle that nearly filled the room. I saw their round black eyes go up to the circle I had formed.

And then I watched them bounce and roll— into a circle!

Were they copying me?

I straightened my fingers and thumbs into a triangle.

And the egg creatures formed a triangle.

Yes!

We're communicating! I realized. We're talking to each other!

I suddenly felt really excited. I felt like some kind of pioneer.

I'm the first person on earth to communicate with Martians! I told myself.

These creatures are friendly, I decided. They're not dangerous.

I didn't really know that for sure. But I was so excited that I had communicated with them, I didn't want to think anything bad about them.

Dr Gray has no right to keep them prisoner here, I thought.

And he has no right to lock me up with them.

I didn't believe his excuse for keeping me here. Not for a minute.

Just because I touched one? Just because I handled one?

Did he really expect me to believe that touching an egg creature could harm me?

Did he really think it would rot my skin off or something?

Did he really think that touching an egg creature would give me a weird disease or change me in some way?

That was just stupid.

I carried the little yellow blob in my hands— and I felt perfectly fine.

These creatures are my friends, I told myself. Touching them isn't going to harm me in any way.

But I'm a scientist. At least, I want to be a scientist. So I have to be scientific, I realized.

I decided to check myself out—just to make sure.

I raised my hands and inspected them carefully, first one, then the other. They looked okay to me. No strange rashes. No skin peeling off. I still had four fingers and a thumb on each hand.

I rubbed my arms. They were the same too. Perfectly okay.

Might as well check myself out all over, I told myself.

I reached down and grabbed my left leg.

Soft and mushy!

"Oh no!" I wailed.

I squeezed my leg again. Soft and lumpy.

I didn't have to look. I knew what was happening.

I was slowly turning into one of them. I was turning into a lump of scrambled eggs!

"No. Oh, please—no."

I squeezed my mushy ankle. I couldn't bear to look down. I didn't want to see what was happening to me.

But I had to.

Slowly, I lowered my gaze.

And saw that I was squeezing one of the egg creatures. Not my leg.

I let go instantly and raised my hand. A relieved laugh escaped my throat.

"Oh wow!"

How could I think that mushy blob was my leg?

I watched the little Martian scurry back to its pals.

I shook my head. Even though no one else was around, I felt like a total jerk.

Just calm down, Dana, I scolded myself.

But how could I?

The air in the lab seemed to get colder. I couldn't

stop shivering. I clamped my jaws tightly. But I couldn't stop my teeth from chattering.

I squeezed my nose. Cold and numb. I rubbed my ears. They were numb too.

This is no joke, I thought, my throat tightening. I'm going to get frostbite. I'm really going to freeze.

I tried thinking warm thoughts. I thought about the beach in summer. I thought about a blazing fire in the fireplace in our den.

It didn't help.

A hard shiver made my whole body twitch.

I've got to do something to take my mind off the cold, I decided.

The egg creatures had spread out over the room. I raised my hands again and formed a triangle.

They stared up at it, but didn't move.

I curled my fingers into a circle.

They ignored this one too.

"I guess you guys got bored, huh?" I asked them.

I tried to bend my fingers and thumbs into a rectangle. But it was too hard. Fingers and thumbs can't really bend into a rectangle.

Besides, the egg creatures weren't paying much attention to me.

I'm going to freeze, I told myself again. Freeze. Freeze. Freeze. The word repeated in my mind until it became an unhappy chant.

I lowered myself to the floor and pressed into the corner. I curled up, trying to save body warmth. Or what was left of it.

A sound on the other side of the window made me jump up.

Someone was coming. Dr Gray? To let me out?

I turned eagerly to the door. I heard footsteps out in the hall. Then a clink of metal.

A slot opened just above the floor to the left of the door. A food tray slid in. It plopped on to the floor.

I hurried over to it. Macaroni and cheese and a small container of milk.

"But I *hate* macaroni and cheese!" I screeched.

No reply.

"I hate it! I hate it! I hate it!" I wailed.

I was starting to lose it again. But I didn't care.

I leaned over the tray and held my hands over the plate of macaroni. The steam warmed my hands.

At least it's hot, I thought.

I sat down on the floor and lifted the tray to my lap. Then I gulped down the macaroni, just for the warmth.

It tasted horrible. I hate that wet, clotted, cheesy taste. But it did warm me up a little.

I didn't open the milk. Too cold.

Feeling a little better, I shoved the tray aside and climbed to my feet. I strode over to the window and started pounding the glass with my fists.

"Dr Gray—let me out!" I shouted. "Dr Gray— I know you can hear me. Let me out! You can't lock me in here and make me eat macaroni and cheese! Let me out!"

I screamed until my voice was hoarse. I didn't hear a reply. Not a sound from the other side of the glass.

I turned away from the window in disgust.

"I've got to find a way out of here," I said out loud. "I've *got* to!"

And then, I had an idea.

Sad to say, it was a bad idea.

The kind of idea you think of when you're freezing to death in a total panic.

What was the idea? To call home and tell Mum and Dad to come and get me.

The only problem with that idea was that there were no phones in the room.

I searched carefully. There were metal shelves up to the ceiling against the back wall. They contained only scientific books and files. There was a desk in one corner. The desktop was bare.

Nothing else.

Nothing else in the whole room. Except for the dozens of egg creatures and me.

I needed another idea, an idea that didn't call for a telephone.

But I was stumped. I tried the door again. I thought Dr Gray might have been careless and left it unlocked.

No such luck.

I checked out the slot where my food tray had been delivered. It was only a few inches tall. Far too narrow for me to slip through.

I was trapped. A prisoner. A specimen.

I dropped glumly down to the floor and rested my back against the wall. I pulled up my knees and wrapped my arms around them. I curled into a ball, trying to stay warm.

How long did Dr Gray plan to keep me here? For ever?

I let out a miserable sigh. But then a thought helped to cheer me. I suddenly had a little hope.

I remembered something I had forgotten. I had told Anne where I was going!

This morning in her back garden, I had told Anne I was going to take the egg creature to the science lab.

I'm going to be rescued! I realized.

I leaped to my feet and shot both fists into the air. I opened my mouth in a happy cheer. "Yesssss!"

I knew exactly what would happen.

When I don't show up for dinner, Mum or Dad will call Anne. Because that's where I'm always hanging out when I should be home for dinner.

Anne will tell them I went to the science lab on Denver.

Mum will say, "He should be back by now."

Dad will say, "I'd better go get him."

And Dad will come and rescue me.

Only a matter of time, I knew. Only a matter of a few hours, and Dad will be here to get me out of this freezer.

I felt so much better.

I lowered myself back to the floor and leaned against the wall to wait. The egg creatures all stared at me. Watched me in silence. Trying to figure me out, I guess.

I didn't realize that I fell asleep. I guess I was worn out from all the excitement—and the fear.

I'm not sure how long I slept.

Voices woke me up. Voices from out in the hall.

I sat up, instantly alert. And I listened.

And heard Dad's voice.

Yes!

He was here. He was about to rescue me.

Yes!

I climbed to my feet. I stretched. I got ready to greet Dad.

And then, from the front hall, I heard Dr Gray say, "I'm sorry, Mr Johnson. Your son never stopped here."

"Are you sure?" I heard Dad ask.

"Very sure," Dr Gray replied. "I'm the only one here today. We're closed. We had no visitors."

"He's about this tall," I heard Dad say. "He has dark hair, and he wears glasses."

"No. Sorry," Dr Gray insisted.

"But he told his friend that he was coming here. He had something he wanted to show to a scientist. His bike is gone from the garage."

"Well, you can check outside for your son's bike," Dr Gray told Dad. "But I don't think you'll find it."

He moved it! I realized. Dr Gray moved my bike so no one would find it!

I let out a shout of rage and ran to the window. "Dad—I'm in here!" I shouted. I cupped my hands around my mouth so my voice would be even louder. "Dad! Can you hear me? I'm in here! Dad?"

I took a deep breath and listened. My heart

was thudding so loudly, I could hardly hear their voices from the front.

Dad and Dr Gray continued talking in low, calm voices.

"Dad! Can't you hear me?" I screamed. "It's me, Dana! Come back here, Dad! I'm here! Come and let me out!"

My voice cracked. My throat ached from screaming so loudly.

"Dad—*please!*"

My chest heaving, I pressed my ear against the window and listened again.

"Well, it's very strange, Mr Johnson," Dr Gray was saying. "The boy never came here. Would you like to look around the lab?"

Yes, Dad! I pleaded silently. *Say yes.*

Tell him that you'd like to look around the lab, Dad! Please!

"No thanks," I heard Dad say. "I'd better keep searching. Thank you, Dr Gray."

I heard Dad say goodbye.

I heard the front door close.

And I knew I was doomed.

"I don't believe this," I murmured out loud. "Dad was so close. So close!"

I sank back to the floor. I felt as if my heart were sinking too. I wanted to keep dropping, down on to the floor, into the ground. Just keep sinking till I disappeared for ever.

My throat ached from screaming. Why couldn't Dad hear me? I could hear him.

And why did he believe Dr Gray's lies? Why didn't Dad check out the lab for himself?

He would see me through the window. And I would be rescued.

Dr Gray is evil, I realized. He pretends to be interested only in science. He pretended to be worried about my health, about my safety. He said that's why he was keeping me here—to make sure I was safe.

But he lied to my father.

And he was lying to me.

Crouched on the floor, I shivered as the frigid air seemed to seep right through my skin. I shut my eyes and lowered my head.

I wanted to stay calm. I knew I had to stay calm to think clearly. But I couldn't. The chills I felt running down my back weren't just from the cold. They were also from terror.

Voices in the front snapped me to attention. I held my breath and listened.

Was that my dad?

Or was I starting to hear things?

"Maybe I *will* take a look around." That's what I thought I heard Dad say.

Was I dreaming it?

No. I heard Dr Gray mumble something. Then I heard Dad say, "Sometimes Dana sneaks into places where he doesn't belong. He's so interested in science, he may have sneaked in through a back door, Dr Gray."

"Yes!" I cried happily. Every time I lost all hope, I somehow got another chance.

I jumped up and hurried to the window. I crossed my fingers and prayed Dad would walk to the back and see me.

After a few seconds, I saw Dad and Dr Gray at the far end of the long, white hall. Dr Gray was leading him slowly, opening doors. They peered into each lab, then moved on.

"Dad!" I called. "Can you hear me? I'm back here!"

Even though I had my face pressed up to the window glass, he couldn't hear me.

I banged on the glass. Dad kept walking with Dr Gray. He didn't look up.

I waited for them to come closer. My heart was banging against my chest now. My mouth was dry. I pressed up close to the window.

In a few seconds, Dad would peer into the window and see me standing here.

And then I would be out—and Dr Gray would have some real explaining to do.

With my hands and nose pressed against the glass, I watched them move forward. The hall was dark on this end. But I could see them clearly as they peeked into the labs at the other end.

"Dad!" I shouted. "Dad—over here!"

I knew he couldn't hear me. But I had to shout anyway.

The two men disappeared into a lab for a few seconds. Then they came out and stepped towards me.

They were talking in low tones. I couldn't hear what they were saying.

Dad had his eyes on Dr Gray.

Turn this way, Dad, I silently urged. *Please— look to the end of the hall. Look in the window.*

Chatting softly, they disappeared through another door.

What on earth are they talking about? I wondered.

A few seconds later, they were back in the hall. Moving this way.

Dad—please! Here I am! I pressed up eagerly against the glass.

I pounded my fists on the window.

Dad looked up.

And stared into the window.

He stared right at me.

I'm rescued! I realized.

I'm *outta* here!

Dad stared at me for a few seconds.

Then he turned back to Dr Gray. "Thanks for showing me around," he said. "Dana definitely isn't here. Sorry I wasted your time."

"Dad—I'm right here!" I shrieked. "You're looking right at me!"

Was I invisible?

Why didn't he see me?

"Sorry I wasted your time, Dr Gray," I heard Dad say again.

"Good luck in finding Dana," Dr Gray replied. "I'm sure he'll turn up really soon. He's probably at a friend's house and forgot the time. You know how kids are."

"Nooooooo!" I let out a long wail. "Dad—come back! Dad!"

As I stared in horror, Dad turned away and started back down the long hall.

With another cry, I began to pound on the window glass with both fists. "Dad! Dad! Dad!" I chanted with each slam of my fist.

Dad turned around. "What's that noise?" he asked Dr Gray.

Dr Gray turned too.

I pounded the glass even harder. I pounded until my knuckles were raw and throbbing. "Dad! Dad! Dad!" I continued to chant.

"What's that pounding noise?" Dad demanded from halfway down the hall.

"It's the pipes," Dr Gray told him. "I've been having a lot of trouble with the pipes. The plumber is coming on Monday."

Dad nodded.

He kept walking. I heard him say goodbye to the scientist. Then I heard the door close behind him.

I knew that this time he wouldn't come back.

I didn't move from the window. I stared through the glass down the long hall.

A few seconds later, I saw Dr Gray coming towards me. He had an angry scowl on his face.

I'm his prisoner now, I thought glumly.

What does he plan to do?

He stopped outside the window. He clicked on the hall light.

In the bright light, I could see beads of sweat on his forehead. He frowned and stared in at me with those cold blue eyes.

"Nice try, Dana," he said sourly.

"Huh? What do you mean?" I choked out. My legs were trembling. Not from the cold. I was really terrified now.

"You almost got your father's attention," Dr Gray replied. "That wouldn't have been nice. That would have spoiled my plans."

I pressed both palms against the glass. I tried to force myself to stop trembling.

"Why couldn't Dad see me?" I demanded.

Dr Gray rubbed a hand over his side of the window. "It's one-way glass," he explained. "No one can see into the room from the hall—unless I turn on the bright hall light."

I let out a long sigh. "You mean—?"

"Your father saw only blackness," the scientist said with a pleased grin. "He thought he was staring into an empty room. Just the way you did—until I turned on the light."

"But why didn't he hear me?" I demanded. "I was shouting my head off."

Dr Gray shook his head. "A waste of time. The room you are in is totally soundproof. Not a sound escapes into the hall."

"But I can hear you!" I declared. "I could hear every word you and Dad said. And now you can hear me."

"There is a speaker system in the wall," he explained. "I can turn it on and off with the same control unit that locks the door."

"So I could hear you, but you couldn't hear me," I murmured.

"You're a very smart boy," he replied. His blue eyes flashed. "I know you're smart enough not to try any more tricks in there."

"You have to let me out!" I screamed. "You can't keep me here!"

"Yes, I can," he replied softly. "I can keep you here as long as I like, Dana."

"But—but—" I sputtered. I was so frightened, I couldn't speak.

"It's my duty to keep you in there," Dr Gray said calmly. He didn't care that I was so scared and upset. He didn't care about me at all, I realized.

He must be crazy, I decided.

Crazy and evil.

"It's my duty to keep you here," he repeated. "I must make sure that the egg creatures haven't harmed you. I must make sure that the egg creatures haven't given you strange germs that you might pass on to others."

"Let me out!" I shrieked. I was too frightened and angry to argue with him now. Too angry and frightened to think clearly. "Let me out! Let me out!" I demanded, pounding on the glass with my aching fists.

"Get some rest, Dana," he instructed. "Don't tire yourself out, son. I want to start doing tests on you in the morning. I have many, many tests to perform."

"But I'm f-freezing!" I stammered. "Let me out of here. At least let me stay somewhere warm. Please?"

He ignored my plea. He clicked off the hall light and turned away.

I watched him make his way down the long hall. He disappeared through a door in front. And closed the door hard behind him.

I stood there, trembling, my heart pounding.

I was cold—and very scared.

I had no way of knowing things were about to get a *lot* scarier!

I was so desperate to get Dad's attention, I nearly forgot about the egg creatures. Now I turned from the window to find them scattered around the room.

They stood still as statues. They didn't bounce or quiver. They all seemed to be staring at me.

Dr Gray had turned off the hall lights except for a tiny, dim bulb in the ceiling. The little egg blobs appeared pale and grey in the dim light.

I felt a chill at the back of my neck.

Was it safe to go to sleep in the same room with them?

I suddenly felt exhausted. So tired that all my muscles ached. My head spun.

I needed sleep.

I knew I had to rest so I could be alert and sharp tomorrow. Alert and sharp so I could find a way to escape.

But if I fell asleep, what would the egg creatures do?

Would they leave me alone? Would they sleep too?

Or would they try to harm me in some way?

Were they good? Were they evil?

Were they intelligent at all?

I had no way of knowing.

I only knew I couldn't stay awake much longer.

I dropped down to the floor and curled up in the corner. I tried to stay warm by tucking myself into a ball.

But it didn't help. The cold swept over me. My nose was frozen. My ears were numb. My glasses were frozen to my face.

Even wrapped up tightly, I couldn't stop shaking.

I'm going to freeze to death, I realized.

When Dr Gray comes back tomorrow morning, he'll find me on the floor. A solid lump of ice.

I gazed at the egg creatures. They stared back at me in the dim light.

Silence.

Such heavy silence in the room that I wanted to scream.

"Aren't you cold?" I cried out to them. My voice came out hoarse, weak from all the screaming I had done. "Aren't you freezing to death too?" I asked them. "How can you guys stand it?"

Of course they didn't reply.

"Dana, you're totally losing it," I scolded myself out loud.

I was trying to talk to a bunch of egg lumps from another planet! Did I really expect them to answer me?

They stared back in silence. None of them quivered. None of them moved. Their little dark eyes glowed in the dim light from the ceiling.

Maybe they're asleep, I thought.

Maybe they sleep with their eyes open. That's why they're not moving. That's why they've stopped bouncing. They're sound asleep.

That made me feel a little better.

I tucked myself into a tighter ball, and I tried to fall asleep too. If only I could stop shivering.

I closed my eyes and silently repeated the word, "sleep, sleep, sleep," in my mind.

It didn't help.

And when I opened my eyes, I saw the egg creatures start to move.

I was wrong. They weren't asleep.

They were wide awake. And they were all moving together. All moving at once.

Coming to get me.

"Ohhh." A low moan escaped from my throat.

I was already shaking all over from the cold. But now my entire body shuddered from fear.

The egg creatures moved with surprising speed.

They were bunching together in the centre of the room. Pressing into each other, making wet smacking sounds.

I tried to climb to my feet. But my legs didn't work.

My knees bent like rubber, and I landed back on the floor. I pressed back into the corner— and watched them move.

They slapped up against each other. Loud, wet slaps.

And as they pushed together, they rolled forward. Rolled towards me.

"What are you doing?" I cried in a high, shrill voice. "What are you going to do to me?"

They didn't reply.

The wet smacks echoed through the room as the egg creatures threw themselves into each other.

"Leave me alone!" I shrieked. Once again I tried to stand. I made it to my knees. But I was trembling too hard to balance on two feet.

"Leave me alone—please! I'll help you guys escape too!" I promised. "Really. I'll help you escape—tomorrow. Just let me make it through the night."

They didn't seem to understand.

They didn't seem to hear me!

What are they doing? I asked myself, watching them creep forward. Why are they doing this?

They had waited until I nearly fell asleep, I realized.

That means they wanted to catch me off guard. They wanted to sneak up on me.

Because they were about to do something I wasn't going to like. Something I wasn't going to like at all.

I pressed my back against the wall.

The egg creatures moved quickly now, pale in the grey light.

Squinting hard at them, I realized to my horror that they had all stuck themselves together.

They were no longer dozens of little egg creatures.

219

Now they had joined together to form *one enormous egg creature*!

I was staring at a big, quivering *wall* of egg! A wall so big it nearly covered the floor of the room.

A wall that was rolling towards me. Rolling to get me.

"Whoa! Please—whoa!" I choked out.

I knew I should climb to my feet. I knew I should try to run.

But where could I run?

How could I escape from this huge, solid egg wall?

I couldn't.

So I lay there and watched it come. Too frozen. Too frozen to move.

"Ohhhh." I moaned as the front of the wall of eggs rose up over my shoes.

It was moving so fast now. Crawling somehow.

Crawling over me.

The egg wall swept over my shoes. Over the legs of my jeans. Over my waist.

I lay there helpless as it swept over me.

Too frozen. Too frozen.

Helpless, as it poured over me.

Trapping me beneath it.

Smothering me.

I should have moved.

I should have fought it.

Too late. Too late now.

The sticky, warm egg creatures—all glued together—rolled over me like a heavy carpet.

I pushed up both arms. I raised my knees. I tried to squirm away.

Too late.

I tried to roll out from underneath. But the heavy, living carpet had me pinned on my back. Pinned to the floor.

It rolled over my waist. And then quickly, over my chest.

Was it going to sweep over my head? Was it going to smother me?

I punched at it with both fists.

But it was too late to push it away. Too late to do it any harm.

Too late to stop it as it crept closer to my neck. So warm and heavy.

I twisted my head from side to side. I tried to roll away.

But it was no use.

Too late. Too late to fight back.

And now I lay there, trapped. And felt it creep up to my chin.

Felt it throbbing. Pulsing.

Dozens of eggy monsters all pressed together. Alive. A living sheet of egg creatures. Covering me.

Covering me.

I took a deep breath and held it as the heavy, warm carpet pressed itself against my chin. My arms and legs were pinned to the floor. I couldn't squirm away.

I couldn't move.

To my surprise, the egg carpet stopped under my chin.

I let out a long whoosh of air.

And waited.

Had it really stopped?

Yes.

It didn't crawl over my head. It rested heavily on top of me. Throbbing steadily, as if it had two dozen heartbeats.

So warm.

I felt so warm beneath it. Almost cosy.

I let out a sigh. For the first time, I had stopped shivering. My hands and feet were no longer frozen. No chills ran down my back.

Warm. I felt toasty and warm.

A smile spread over my face. I could feel my fear fading away with the cold.

The egg creatures weren't trying to harm me, I realized.

They wanted to help me.

They pressed themselves together to form a blanket. A warm and cosy blanket.

They worked together to keep me from freezing.

They saved my life!

With the warm, pulsing blanket on top of me, I suddenly felt calm. And sleepy. I drifted into a peaceful, dreamless sleep.

Such a wonderful, soothing sleep.

But it didn't help get me ready for the horrors of the next morning.

I awoke a couple of times during the night. At first, I felt alarmed and frightened when I saw that I wasn't home in bed.

But the pulsing, warm egg blanket relaxed me. I shut my eyes and drifted back to sleep.

Some time in the morning, I was aroused from a deep sleep by an angry voice. I felt hands grab my shoulders roughly.

Someone was shaking me hard. Shaking me awake.

I opened my eyes to find Dr Gray bending over me in his white lab coat. His face was twisted in anger. He shook me hard, shouting furiously.

"Dana—what have you done? What have you done to the egg monsters?"

"Huh?" I was still half asleep. My eyes struggled to focus. My head bobbed loosely on my shoulders as the angry scientist shook me.

"Let me go!" I finally managed to choke out.

"What have you done to them?" Dr Gray

demanded. "How did you turn them into a blanket?"

"I—I didn't!" I stammered.

He uttered a furious growl. "You've ruined everything!" he shrieked.

"Please—" I started, struggling to wake up.

He let go of me and grabbed the egg blanket in both hands. "What have you done, Dana?" he repeated. "Why did you do this?"

With another cry of rage, he ripped the blanket off me—and heaved it against the wall.

The egg creatures made a soft *splat* as they hit the lab wall. I heard them utter tiny squeals of pain. The blanket folded limply to the floor.

"You shouldn't do that, Dr Gray!" I screamed, finally finding my voice. I jumped to my feet. I could still feel the warmth of the egg blanket on my skin.

"You hurt them!" I shrieked.

I gazed down at the yellow blanket. It bubbled silently where it had been thrown. It didn't move.

"You let them touch you?" Dr Gray demanded, twisting his face in disgust. "You let them cover you up?"

"They saved my life!" I declared. "They pushed together to make a warm blanket—and they saved my life!"

I glanced down again. The egg creatures remained stuck together. The blanket appeared to be seething now. Throbbing hard. As if excited. Or angry.

"Are you crazy?" Dr Gray cried, his face red with anger. "Are you crazy? You let these *monsters* rest on top of you? You touched them? You handled them? Are you trying to destroy my discovery? Are you trying to destroy my work?"

He's the crazy one, I realized. Dr Gray isn't making any sense. He isn't making any sense at all.

He moved quickly—and grabbed me again. Held me in a tight grip so I couldn't escape. And pulled me to the door.

"Let go of me! Where are you taking me?" I demanded.

"I thought you could be trusted," Dr Gray replied in a menacing growl. "But I was wrong. I'm so sorry, Dana. So sorry. I had hoped to keep you alive. But I see now that is impossible."

He dragged me to the door. He stopped and reached into the pocket of his lab coat. Reached for the control unit to open the door.

I saw my chance. He had me by only one hand. With a hard burst of strength, I pulled away. He let out a cry. Reached both hands for me. Missed.

I ran to the other side of the lab. I turned at the wall to face him.

He had a strange smile on his face. "Dana, there's nowhere to run," he said softly.

My eyes flashed around the room. I don't know what I was searching for. I had seen it all. And I knew that he was telling the truth.

Dr Gray stood blocking the only door. The long window was too heavy and thick to break through. And it didn't open.

There were no other windows. No other doors. No ways to escape.

"What are you going to do now, Dana?" Dr

Gray asked softly, the strange smile stuck on his face. His blue eyes locked coldly on mine. "Where are you going to go?"

I opened my mouth to reply. But I had nothing to say.

"I'll tell you what's going to happen," Dr Gray said softly, calmly. "You're going to stay in here. In this cold, cold room. I'm going to leave you now and make sure you're locked in."

His smile grew wider. "Then do you know what I'm going to do? Do you?"

"What?" I choked out.

"I'm going to make it colder in here. I'm going to make it colder than a freezer."

"No—!" I protested.

His smile faded. "I trusted you, Dana. I trusted you. But you broke that trust. You let them touch you. You let them form this—this carpet! You ruined them, Dana! You ruined my egg monsters!"

"I—I didn't do anything!" I stammered. I balled my hands into fists. But I felt so helpless. Helpless and afraid.

"You can't freeze me in here!" I cried. "I didn't do anything! You can't leave me in here to freeze!"

"Of course I can," Dr Gray replied coldly. "This is my lab. My own little world. I can do whatever I want."

He pulled the little black remote unit from his

lab coat pocket. He pointed it at the door and pushed a button.

The door swung open.

He started to leave. "Goodbye, Dana," he called.

"No—stop!" I called.

Dr Gray turned from the doorway.

And as he turned, the blanket of egg creatures rose up.

It stood straight up—and flung itself over him. It dropped on top of the scientist with a hard *thud*.

"Hey—" He let out an angry cry. The cry was muffled by the heavy yellow blanket of egg creatures.

The egg blanket covered him. I watched him struggle underneath it. And I listened to his muffled cries.

He was squirming and twisting beneath the blanket. But he couldn't toss it off. And he couldn't slide out from under it.

He crumpled to the floor, and the blanket crumpled with him.

I watched it seething and bubbling on top of him.

Then I didn't wait another second. I took a deep breath—and I ran across the room. I darted past the egg blanket with Dr Gray twisting and thrashing underneath it.

Out the door.

Down the long hall to the front of the lab.

Yes! A few seconds later, I pushed open the front door and burst outside. Breathing hard, sucking in the sweet, fresh air.

A beautiful morning. A red ball of a sun still rising over the spring-green trees. The sky clear and blue.

I glanced around. I could see a paper-boy on his bike halfway up the block. No one else on the street.

I turned and ran around to the side of the building. The grass smelled so wonderful! The morning air so warm and fresh. I was so thrilled to be outside!

I had to get home.

I had a hunch—and the hunch was right. I spotted my bike, resting against the back wall of the lab, hidden by a large rubbish bin.

I leapt on to it and started to pedal. Riding a bike never felt as exciting, so *thrilling*!

I was getting away, away from the horror of crazy Dr Gray and his freezing lab.

I pedalled faster. I rode without stopping. Without *seeing*! The world was a blur of green.

I must have set a speed record for getting

home. I roared up the driveway, the tyres sending gravel flying on both sides.

Then I jumped off my bike and let it topple to the grass. I dived for the kitchen door and burst into the kitchen. "Mum!" I cried.

She jumped up from the breakfast table. I caught the worried expression on her face. It melted away as I ran into the room.

"Dana!" she cried. "Where *were* you? We've all been so terrified. The police are looking for you and—and—"

"I'm okay!" I told her. I gave her a quick hug.

Dad ran in from the hallway. "Dana—you're okay? Where *were* you all night? Your mother and I—"

"Egg monsters!" I cried. "Egg monsters from Mars! Hurry!" I grabbed Dad's hand and tugged. "Come on!"

"Huh?" Dad spun around. He narrowed his eyes, studying me. "What did you say?"

"No time to explain!" I gasped. "They've got Dr Gray. He's evil, Dad. He's so evil!"

"Who has *what*?" Mum demanded.

"The egg creatures! From Mars! Hurry! There's no time!"

They didn't move. I saw them exchange glances.

Mum stepped forward and placed a hand on my forehead. "Do you have a fever, Dana? Are you sick?"

"No!" I screamed. "Listen to me! Egg creatures from Mars! Follow me!"

I know I wasn't explaining myself too well. But I was frantic.

"Dana—come and lie down," Mum instructed. "I'll call Dr Martin."

"No—please! I don't need a doctor!" I protested. "Just follow me—okay? You've got to see them. You've got to see the egg creatures. You've got to hurry."

Mum and Dad exchanged worried glances again.

"I'm not crazy!" I shrieked. "I want you to come with me to the science lab!"

"Okay, okay," Dad finally agreed. "You were in that lab last night?"

"Yes," I told him, shoving him to the kitchen door. "I called and called. But you couldn't hear me."

"Oh, wow," Dad murmured, shaking his head. "Wow."

The three of us climbed into the car.

It took about three minutes to drive to the lab. Dad parked in front. I jumped out of the car before he stopped.

The front door to the lab stood wide open, as I'd left it.

I ran inside with Mum and Dad close behind me.

"They're egg creatures," I told them breathlessly. "They dropped down from Mars. They captured Dr Gray."

I led the way down the long hall.

I pushed open the door to the freezing back room.

Mum and Dad stepped in behind me.

I gazed around the room—and gasped in amazement!

I saw Mum and Dad staring at me. They had worried expressions on their faces.

"Where are the egg creatures?" Mum demanded softly.

Dad rested a hand gently on my shoulder. "Where are they, Dana?" he asked in a whisper.

"Uh . . . they're gone," I choked out.

The lab stood empty.

No Dr Gray. No egg creatures. No one.

Bare white walls. Nothing on the floor.

Nothing.

"Maybe they went back to Mars," I murmured, shaking my head.

"And Dr Gray? What about Dr Gray?" Dad asked.

"Maybe they took Dr Gray with them," I replied.

"Let's go home," Mum sighed. "Let's get you into bed, Dana."

Dad guided me from the room, his hands on

my shoulders. "I'll call Dr Martin," he said softly. "I'm sure we can get him to come to the house this morning."

"I—I do feel a little strange," I admitted.

So they drove me home and tucked me into bed.

The doctor came later that morning and examined me. He didn't find anything wrong. But he said I should stay in bed and rest for a while.

I knew that Mum and Dad didn't believe my story. I felt bad about that. But I didn't know how to convince them I was telling the truth.

I did feel a little weird.

Just tired, I guess.

I dozed off and woke up and dozed off again.

In the afternoon, I woke up to hear my sister Brandy talking to some friends outside my room. "Dana totally freaked out," I heard Brandy say. "He says he was kidnapped by egg monsters from Mars."

I heard Brandy's friends giggling.

Oh great, I thought bitterly. Now everyone thinks I'm a nut case.

I wanted to call Brandy into my room and tell her what really happened. I wanted to make her believe me. I wanted to make *someone* believe me.

But how?

I fell asleep again.

I was awakened by a voice calling my name. I sat up in bed. The voice floated in from my open bedroom window.

I climbed out of bed and made my way to the window. Anne was calling me from the driveway. "Dana—are you okay? Do you want to come over? I've got a new CD-ROM version of *Battle Chess*."

"Cool!" I called down to Anne. "I'll be right over."

I pulled on a T-shirt and a pair of jeans. I was feeling pretty good. Rested. Like my old self.

So happy that everything was back to normal.

I hummed to myself as I brushed my hair. I stared at myself in the mirror.

You had an amazing adventure, Dana, I told myself. Imagine—you spent the night with egg creatures from Mars!

But now you're okay, and your life is back to normal.

I felt so happy, I gave Brandy a hug on my way down the stairs. She stared at me as if I truly were crazy!

Humming loudly, I made my way out the kitchen door and started across the garden to Anne's house.

Everything looked so beautiful to me. The grass. The trees. The spring flowers. The sun setting behind the trees.

What a day! What a beautiful, perfect, normal day!

And then halfway across Anne's lawn, I stopped.

I crouched down on the grass—and I laid the biggest egg you ever saw!

Goosebumps

The Beast From
The East

When I was a really little girl, my mum would tuck me into bed at night. She would whisper, "Good night, Ginger. Good night. Don't let the bedbugs bite."

I didn't know what bedbugs were. I pictured fat red bugs with big eyes and spidery legs, crawling under the sheet. Just thinking about them made me itchy all over.

After Mum had kissed me on the forehead and left, Dad would step into my room and sing to me. Very softly. The same song every night. "The Teddy Bears' Picnic."

I don't know why he thought that song made a good lullaby. It was about going into the woods and finding hundreds and hundreds of bears.

The song gave me the shivers. What were the bears eating at their picnic? Children?

After Dad kissed me on the forehead and left the room, I'd be itching and shaking for hours.

Then I'd have nightmares about bedbugs and bears.

Until a few years ago, I was afraid to go into the woods.

I'm twelve now, and I'm not scared any longer.

At least, I wasn't scared until our family camping trip this summer. That's when I discovered that there are a lot scarier creatures than bears in the woods!

But I guess I'd better begin at the beginning.

The first thing I remember about our camping trip is Dad yelling at my brothers. I have two ten-year-old brothers—Pat and Nat. You guessed it. They're twins.

Lucky me—huh?

Pat and Nat aren't just twins. They're identical twins. They look so much alike, they confuse *each other*!

They are both short and skinny. They both have round faces and big brown eyes. They both wear their brown hair parted in the middle and straight down the sides. They both wear baggy, faded jeans and black-and-red skater T-shirts with slogans no one can understand.

There is only one way to tell Pat from Nat or Nat from Pat. You have to ask them who they are!

I remember that our camping trip began on a beautiful, sunny day. The air smelled piney and fresh. Twigs and dead leaves crackled under our shoes as we followed a twisting path through the woods.

Dad led the way. He carried the tent over his shoulder, and he had a bulging backpack on his back. Mum followed him. She was also loaded down with stuff we needed.

The path led through a grassy clearing. The sun felt hot on my face. My backpack began to feel heavy. I wondered how much deeper into the woods Mum and Dad wanted to go.

Pat and Nat followed behind us. Dad kept turning around to yell at them. We all had to yell at Pat and Nat. Otherwise, they never seemed to hear us. They only heard each other.

Why was Dad yelling?

Well, for one thing, Nat kept disappearing. Nat likes to climb trees. If he sees a good tree, he climbs it. I think he's part chimpanzee.

I tell him that as often as I can. Then he scratches his chest and makes chimp noises. He thinks he's really funny.

So there we were, hiking through the woods. And every time we turned around, Nat would be up a tree somewhere. It was slowing us down. So Dad had to yell at him.

Then Dad had to yell at Pat because of his Game Boy. "I told you not to bring that thing!" Dad shouted. Dad is big and broad, kind of like a bear. And he has a booming voice.

It doesn't do him much good. Pat and Nat never listen to him.

Pat walked along, eyes on his Game Boy, his fingers hammering the controls.

"Why are we hiking in the woods?" Dad asked him. "You could be home in your room doing that. Put it away, Pat, and check out the scenery."

"I can't, Dad," Pat protested. "I can't quit now. I'm on Level Six! I've never made it to Level Six before!"

"There goes a chipmunk," Mum chimed in, pointing. Mum is the wildlife guide. She points out everything that moves.

Pat didn't raise his eyes from his Game Boy.

"Where's Nat?" Dad demanded, his eyes searching the clearing.

"Up here, Dad," Nat called. I shielded my eyes with one hand and saw him on a high branch of a tall oak tree.

"Get down from there!" Dad shouted. "That branch won't hold you!"

"Hey—I made it to Level Seven!" Pat declared, fingering frantically.

"Look—two bunny rabbits!" Mum cried. "See them in the tall grass?"

"Let's keep walking," I groaned. "It's too hot here." I wanted to get out of the clearing and back under the cool shade of the trees.

"Ginger is the only sensible one," Dad said, shaking his head.

244

"Ginger is a freak!" Nat called, sliding down from the oak tree.

We made our way through the woods. I don't know how long we walked. It was so beautiful! So peaceful. Beams of sunlight poked through the high branches, making the ground sparkle.

I found myself humming that song about the bears in the woods. I don't know what made it pop into my head. Dad hadn't sung it to me in years and years.

We stopped for lunch by a clear, trickling stream. "This would make a nice camping spot," Mum suggested. "We can set up the tent on the grass here by the shore."

Mum and Dad started to unpack the equipment and set up the tent. I helped them. Pat and Nat threw stones into the stream. Then they got into a wrestling match and tried to shove each other into the water.

"Take them into the woods," Dad instructed me. "Try to lose them—okay?"

He was joking, of course.

He had no way of knowing that, Pat, Nat and I would soon be lost for real—with little hope of ever returning.

"What do you want to do?" Nat demanded. He had picked up a thin tree branch to use as a walking stick. Pat kept slapping at it, trying to make Nat stumble.

We had followed the stream for a while. I saw a million tiny, silver minnows swimming near the surface. Now we were making our own path through the tangle of trees, low shrubs and rocks.

"Hide-and-seek!" Pat declared. He slapped Nat. "You're It!"

Nat slapped him back. "You're It."

"You're It!"

"You're It!"

"You're It!"

The slaps kept getting harder.

"I'll be It!" I cried. Anything to keep them from murdering each other. "Hurry. Go and hide. But don't go too far."

I leaned against a tree, shut my eyes and

started to count to one hundred. I could hear them scampering into the trees.

After thirty, I counted by tens. I didn't want to give them too big a head start. "Ready or not, here I come!" I called.

I found Pat after only a few minutes. He had crouched behind a large white mound of sand. He thought he was hidden. But I spotted his brown hair poking up over the top of the sand.

I tagged him easily.

Nat was harder to find. He had climbed a tree, of course. He was way up at the top, completely hidden by thick clumps of green leaves.

I never would have found him if he hadn't spat on me.

"Get down, creep!" I shouted angrily. I waved a fist up at him. "You're disgusting! Get down— right now!"

He giggled and peered down at me. "Did I hit you?"

I didn't answer. I waited for him to climb down to the ground. Then I rubbed a handful of dried leaves in his face until he was sputtering and choking.

Just a typical Wald family hide-and-seek game.

After that, we chased a squirrel through the woods. The poor thing kept glancing back at us as if he didn't believe we were chasing after him.

He finally got tired of the race and scurried up a tall pine tree.

I glanced around. The trees in this part of the woods grew close together. Their leaves blocked most of the sunlight. The air felt cooler here. In their shade, it was nearly as dark as evening.

"Let's go back," I suggested. "Mum and Dad might be getting worried."

The boys didn't argue. "Which way?" Nat asked.

I glanced around, making a complete circle with my eyes. "Uh ... that way." I pointed. I was guessing. But I felt ninety-nine per cent sure.

"Are you sure?" Pat asked. He eyed me suspiciously. I could see he was a little worried. Pat didn't like the outdoors as much as Nat and me.

"Sure I'm sure," I told him.

I led the way. They followed close behind. They had both picked up walking sticks. After we had walked a few minutes, they started fighting a duel with them.

I ignored them. I had my own worries. I wasn't sure we were walking in the right direction. In fact, I felt totally turned around.

"Hey—there's the stream!" I cried happily.

I immediately felt better. We weren't lost. I had picked the right direction.

Now all we had to do was follow the stream back to the clearing where we had set up camp.

I began to hum again. The boys tossed their sticks into the stream. We began to jog along the grassy shore.

"Whoa!" I cried out when my left boot started to sink. I nearly fell into a deep mud patch. I pulled my hiking boot up. Soaked in wet, brown mud up over the ankle.

Pat and Nat thought that was a riot. They laughed and slapped each other high fives.

I growled at them, but I didn't waste any words. They're both hopeless. So totally immature.

Now I couldn't wait to get back to camp and clean the thick mud off my boot. We jogged along the shore, then cut through the skinny, white-trunked trees and into the clearing.

"Mum! Dad!" I called, hurrying over the grass. "We're back!"

I stopped so short, both boys tumbled into me.

My eyes searched the clearing.

"Mum? Dad?"

They were gone.

"They left us!" Pat exclaimed. He ran frantically around the clearing. "Mum! Dad!"

"Earth to Pat," Nat called. He waved his hand in front of Pat's face. "We're in the wrong place, you wimp."

"Nat is right," I replied, glancing around. There were no footprints, no tent markers. We were in a different clearing.

"I thought you knew the way, Ginger," Pat complained. "Didn't they teach you anything at that nature camp?"

Nature camp! Last summer my parents forced me to spend two weeks at an "Explore the Great Outdoors" camp. I got poison ivy the first day. After that, I didn't listen to anything the counsellors said.

Now I wished I had.

"We should have left markers on the trees," I said, "to find our way back."

"*Now* you think of it?" Nat groaned, rolling

his eyes. He picked up a long, crooked stick and waved it in my face.

"Give me that," I ordered.

Nat handed me the stick. Yellow sap oozed on to my palm. It smelled sour.

"Gross!" I shouted. I tossed the stick away. I rubbed my hands on my jeans. But the yellow stain wouldn't come off my palm.

That's weird, I thought. I wondered what the stuff was. I definitely didn't like it on my skin.

"Let's follow the stream," I suggested. "Mum and Dad can't be too far."

I tried to sound calm. But I was totally twisted around. In fact, I had no idea where we were.

We headed out of the clearing and back to the shore. The sun fell lower in the sky. It prickled the back of my neck.

Pat and Nat tossed pebbles into the water. After a few minutes, they tossed them at each other.

I ignored them. At least they weren't throwing anything at me.

As we walked along, the air became cooler. The path grew narrower.

The water turned dark and murky. Silvery-blue fish snapped at the air. The skinny branches of the tall trees reached down towards us.

A feeling of dread swept over me. Nat and Pat

grew quiet. They actually stopped picking on each other.

"I don't remember any of these bushes near our campsite," Pat said nervously. He pointed to a short, squat plant. Its strange blue leaves looked like open umbrellas stacked one on top of the other. "Are you sure we're going the right way?"

By now I was sure we *weren't* heading in the right direction. I didn't remember those strange bushes, either.

Then we heard a noise on the other side of the shrubs.

"Maybe that's Mum and Dad!" Pat exclaimed.

We pushed our way through the plants. And ran into another *deserted* clearing.

I glanced around. This grassy field was enormous. Large enough for a hundred tents.

My heart hammered against my chest.

We stood on rust-coloured grass. It stuck up over my ankle. A clump of gigantic purple cabbage plants grew to our right.

"This place is cool!" Nat cried. "Everything is so big."

To me, the clearing wasn't cool at all. It gave me the creeps.

Strange trees surrounded us on all sides. Their branches shot out at right angles to the trunk. They resembled stairs going up and up and up. Up into the clouds.

They were the tallest trees I'd ever seen. And perfect for climbing.

Red moss clung to the branches. Yellow gourds hung from braided vines, swaying in the air.

Where were we? This looked like a weird jungle—not the woods! Why were all the trees and plants so strange?

A knot formed in the pit of my stomach.

Where was our clearing? Where were Mum and Dad?

Nat jogged over to a tree. "I'm climbing up," he said.

"No, you don't," I protested. I rushed over and pulled his arm from the branch.

The red moss rubbed against my palm. My skin turned red where I touched it. Now I had a yellow-and-red design on my hand.

What's going on here? I wondered.

Before I could show my hand to my brothers, the tree started to shake.

"Whoa! Watch out!" I cried.

A small furry animal jumped out of the branches and landed at my feet. I had never seen anything like it before. It was the size of a chipmunk, brown all over except for a white patch around one eye.

It had a bushy tail and floppy ears like a bunny. And two big front teeth like a beaver. Its flat nose twitched. It stared at me with grey eyes, round with fear. I watched it scurry away.

"What was that?" Pat asked.

I shrugged. I wondered what other kinds of weird creatures lived in these woods.

"I'm kind of scared," Pat admitted, huddling close to me.

I felt scared too. But I knew I was the big sister. So I told him everything was okay.

Then I glanced down. "Nat! Pat!" I shouted. "Look!"

My muddy boot stood inside a footprint three times the size of mine. No—even bigger. What kind of animal had a footprint that huge?

A bear? A giant gorilla?

I didn't have time to think about it.

The ground started to tremble.

"Do you feel that?" I asked my brothers.

"It's Dad!" Pat shouted.

It definitely was not Dad. He's a big guy. But no way could he make the ground shake that way!

I heard grumbles and growls from somewhere in the distance. And then a roar. Twigs and branches snapped loudly in the air.

All three of us gasped as a tall beast stomped through the trees. It was huge. So tall that its head touched the middle branches.

It had a narrow, pointy head over a long neck. Its eyes shone like bright green marbles. Shaggy blue fur covered every part of its body. Its long, furry tail thumped heavily on the ground.

The weirdest creature I'd ever seen in my life!

The beast entered the far side of the clearing.

I sucked in my breath as it drew closer. Close enough for me to see its long snout. Its nostrils flared in and out as it sniffed the air.

My brothers hung back, hiding behind me. We huddled together. Trembling.

The beast opened its mouth. Two rows of sharp yellow teeth rose up from purple gums. One long, jagged fang slid down over the creature's chin.

I crouched on my hands and knees. Pulled my brothers down with me.

The beast spun around in circles. It sniffed the air and wiggled its hairy, pointed ears. Had it smelled us? Was it searching for us?

I couldn't think. I couldn't move.

The beast turned its ugly head. It stared at me.

It saw me.

My eyes on the creature, I grabbed my brothers by their T-shirts. I dragged them behind some of the huge cabbage plants.

The beast stayed on the other side of the clearing, sniffing the air. It stomped back and forth, sniffing hard. The ground seemed to shake each time one of its furry paws hit the ground. I could feel Nat and Pat shiver with fear.

The beast turned away from us.

Whew! I thought. It hasn't seen us. I bit my bottom lip and held on to Pat and Nat.

"*Argggh*," the beast grunted. It dropped to all fours. It pressed its snout to the ground and crept along, making loud snuffling noises.

I didn't tell Pat or Nat what I was thinking. The beast hadn't seen us—but there was no way we could keep it from smelling us.

Its long tail swished back and forth. The tail banged against the trees. Gourds fell to the ground.

The beast crawled into the centre of the clearing. Closer.

I dug my fingernails into my palm.

Turn around, beast, I prayed. Go back into the woods. The blue creature stopped. It sniffed again. And then it turned. It began to creep in our direction.

I swallowed. Hard. My mouth suddenly felt so dry.

The creature's tail pushed against one of the cabbage plants near us. The leaves rustled.

"Get down!" I whispered, shoving my brothers. We stretched out flat on the ground.

The beast stopped a few feet from our hiding place.

Its tail brushed my arm. The fur felt rough and scratchy.

I jerked my arm away. Could he feel me? Was I like a tiny animal to him? One he could pick up and squeeze the way my brothers teased our dog?

The beast rose up on its hind legs and sniffed. It towered over the cabbage plant. It had to be at least eight feet tall!

It picked at its fur with a clawed thumb—and placed whatever it found in his mouth.

A pleased grin formed under its twitching snout. It peered around the clearing.

Don't look down, I prayed. Don't see us.

My body tensed.

The creature growled and ran its long tongue over its fang. Then it tromped off into the trees.

I let out a sigh of relief.

"We'd better wait a few minutes," I told my brothers. I counted to one hundred. Then I crawled out from behind the plant. No sign of the creature.

But then I felt the earth shake.

"Oh, no!" I gasped. "Here it comes again!"

The beast's enormous blue head bobbed up between the trees. How had it come back so fast? And from the other direction?

We scrambled back to our hiding place behind the huge cabbage plant.

"We have to get away from here," I whispered. "If it keeps searching back and forth, it's bound to find us."

"How do we get away?" Nat demanded.

I picked up a gourd from the ground. "I'll throw this gourd. The beast will turn its head to see what the noise is. Then we'll run—in the other direction."

"But, what if it sees us? What if it chases us?" Nat asked. He didn't seem happy about my plan.

Nat and Pat exchanged nervous glances.

"Yeah. What if it runs faster than us?" Pat demanded.

"It won't," I said. I was bluffing. But my brothers didn't know that.

I peeked over the top of the cabbage. The creature stood closer than ever. It sniffed the air, its pink snout coiling like a snake.

I glanced at the gourd in my hand, then brought my arm back, ready to throw.

"Wait!" Pat whispered. "Look!"

My arm froze where it was. Another beast had tromped into the clearing.

And another.

And another.

I gulped. More blue beasts clomped into the clearing.

No way could we make a run for it now.

The enormous creatures tromped around the clearing. They growled and grunted to each other.

One stopped and jabbered loudly in a deep and gravelly voice. The folds of hairless skin under its chin wobbled back and forth.

"Look at them all!" Nat murmured. "There must be at least two dozen."

A small beast jogged into the clearing. Its fur shone a brighter blue than the rest. It stood only about three feet tall.

Was it a child? A young beast?

The tiny beast placed its short, pink snout on the ground and sniffed. Dirt and dried-up bits of leaves stuck to its snout.

"It looks hungry," Pat whispered.

"Shhh!" I warned.

The tiny beast glanced up eagerly. In our direction.

It *did* look hungry. But for what?

I held my breath.

The small beast suddenly scooped a gourd off the ground. It shoved the whole thing into its mouth and crunched down. Yellow juice squirted between its lips and soaked down its shaggy blue fur.

It eats fruit! I cheered silently. That was a good sign. Maybe they are vegetarians, I thought. Maybe they don't eat meat.

I knew that most wild animals ate only one type of food. Either meat, or else fruits and vegetables.

Except for bears, I suddenly remembered. Bears will eat both.

A large beast thudded over to the kid. It yanked the little creature to its feet and began jabbering angrily at it. It dragged the kid back towards the woods.

The beast with the hairless folds of skin stepped into the centre of the clearing.

"*Grrugh!*" It snorted at the others. It waved a furry paw in a circle. It waved and grunted and jabbered.

The other creatures nodded and grunted to one another. They seemed to understand each other. They seemed to be grunting some kind of language.

The big beast gave a final grunt. The other creatures turned back towards the woods. They spread out and began to creep silently into the trees. I felt the earth trembling under the pounding of their feet. Twigs and leaves crackled and cracked.

In a few seconds, they had vanished. The clearing stood empty.

I let out another long sigh of relief.

"What are they doing, anyway?" Pat asked.

Nat wiped sweat off his forehead. "They act as if they're searching for something," he answered. "Hunting."

I swallowed hard.

I knew what they were hunting for.

They were hunting for *us*.

And now there were so many of them. Spreading out in every direction.

We don't stand a chance, I realized.

They're going to catch us.

And then what?

I stood up slowly. I turned in a full circle, checking everywhere for a sign of the hairy creatures.

Their low grumbles and growls faded into the distance. The ground stopped shaking.

A gust of cool wind blew through the clearing. It made the gourds in the trees knock against each other. An eerie melody whistled through the trees.

I shuddered.

"Let's get out of here. Now!" Nat cried.

"Wait!" I told him. I grabbed his arm and held him back. "Those beasts are too near. They'll hear us or see us."

"Yeah, well, I'm not going to stick around. I'm going to run as hard as I can. I'm outta here!"

"I'm with you." Pat leaped to his feet. "But which way do we go?" he asked.

"We can't go anywhere now," I argued. "We're lost. We don't know which way to go. So we have

263

to stay right here. Mum and Dad will come and find us. I know they will."

"And what if they don't? What if they're in trouble, too?" Nat asked.

"Dad knows how to survive in the woods," I said firmly. "And we don't."

At least I didn't. If only I had listened at that outdoors camp.

"I do, too!" Pat whined. "I can take care of myself. Right Nat? Let's get going!"

Who was he kidding? Pat didn't even *like* the woods.

But he's stubborn. When he gets an idea, no one can change his mind. And Nat always agrees with him. Twins!

"Ginger—are you coming or not?" Pat demanded.

"You're crazy," I told him. "We have to stay here. That's the rule, remember?"

Mum and Dad always told us, if we ever get lost, stay where we are.

"But there are only two of Mum and Dad— and there's three of us," Pat argued. "So we should go and find them."

"But they're not the ones who are lost!" I cried.

"I think we should go," Pat repeated. "We have to get away from those ugly creatures!"

"Okay," I told them. "We'll go. At least we'll be together."

I still thought they were wrong. But I couldn't

let them go off without me. What if something horrible happened to them?

Besides, I didn't want to stay in these strange woods alone.

As I turned to follow them, I glimpsed something move in the tall grass.

"It's . . . it's . . . them!" Nat stammered. "They're back!"

I stared at the grass in horror.

"Run!" Pat shrieked. He bolted across the clearing.

A squirrel scurried out of the grass.

"Pat, wait!" Nat yelled.

"It's only a squirrel!" I shouted.

He didn't hear us.

Nat and I took off, chasing after Pat.

"Pat! Hey—Pat!"

I didn't see the thick, twisted root that poked out of the ground. I tripped over it and hit the ground hard. I lay there stunned.

Nat knelt down beside me. He grabbed my arm and helped me to my feet.

I glanced up ahead. Pat had already vanished into the woods. I couldn't see him anywhere.

"We have to catch up with him," I told Nat breathlessly. I straightened up, brushing dirt off my knees.

The earth started to tremble again.

"Oh no!" Nat moaned.

The creatures were back.

265

I whirled around. Big blue beasts pushed back through the trees. I counted four behind us. Three on my left. Five to our right.

I gave up counting.

There were too many of them.

The big one grunted and raised its furry paws high in the air. It pointed at us. The other creatures grunted and uttered cries of excitement.

"They've caught us!" I groaned.

"Ginger . . ." Nat whimpered. His eyes opened wide with terror. I clutched at his hand and held it tight.

The beasts drew closer. And formed a circle around us.

Nowhere to run now.

"We're trapped," I whispered.

The beasts began to growl.

Over the drone of their low growls, I heard the eerie melody whistling through the gourds again.

Nat huddled close to me. "They've got us," he whispered. "Do you think—do you think they got Pat?"

I couldn't answer. I couldn't talk.

I felt weak and helpless. Sweat ran down my face into my eyes. I wanted to wipe the sweat away, but I couldn't lift my hand to do it.

I was too scared to move.

Then the beast with the flabby chin stepped forward. It stopped a few inches away from me.

I slowly raised my eyes. I stared at its furry belly. Then its broad chest. I saw shiny, black insects crawling in its fur.

I raised my eyes to its face. Its green eyes glared down at me. It opened its mouth. I stared helplessly at its long fang, chipped on the end.

You don't need a tooth like that for eating *fruit*! I thought.

The beast stretched to its full height. It raised a furry paw high above us. Ready to strike.

Nat huddled closer to me. I could practically feel his heart beating through his T-shirt. Or maybe it was my own heart that was pounding.

The creature growled and swung.

I squeezed my eyes shut.

I felt a slap on my shoulder—so hard it knocked me backwards.

"You're It!" the creature bellowed.

Huh? My mouth dropped open in astonishment.

"You're It," the beast repeated.

I gaped at Nat. His eyes bulged in surprise.

"It . . . it talked!" Nat stammered to me. "In our language."

The creature scowled at Nat. "I talk in many languages," he growled. "We have a universal language adaptor."

"Oh," Nat said weakly. He and I exchanged stunned glances.

The creature growled again and took a step closer to me. "Did you hear me?" he growled. "You're It!"

His marble eyes glared into mine. He tapped a paw impatiently on the ground.

"What do you mean?" I asked.

The creature grunted. "You're the Beast from the East," he said.

"What are you talking about? I'm not a beast. I'm a girl!" I declared. "Ginger Wald."

"I am Fleg," the beast replied, pounding himself on the chest. He waved a paw at the creature beside him, a beast with one eye missing. "This is Spork," Fleg announced. Fleg pounded the other beast on the back.

Spork grunted at Nat and me. I stared at his dark empty eye socket. And I spotted a deep black scar on the side of Spork's nose.

An eye missing and a scar. The big creature had been in a pretty nasty fight. I hoped it wasn't a fight with a human. Because if Spork was the winner, I would hate to see the loser!

Nat gaped at Spork.

"Uh, this is my brother, Nat," I said quickly.

Spork growled in reply.

"Have you seen our mum and dad?" I asked Fleg. "See, we're all here camping, and we got separated. But we're trying to get back together and go home. So, we'd better go—"

"There are others?" Fleg glanced sharply around the clearing. "Where?"

"That's the problem," Nat answered. "We can't find them."

Fleg grunted. "If you can't find them, they can't play."

"Right. That's the rule," Spork agreed. He scratched at the insects that climbed around in his fur.

"Now start moving," Fleg demanded. "It's getting late. And you're It."

I stared at Nat. This was too weird. What did he mean—*they can't play*? And why did he keep saying I was It? Did they want to play tag or something?

The circle of beasts began stomping their paws, shaking the forest ground. "Play . . . play . . ." they chanted.

"Play what?" I demanded. "Is this really some kind of game?"

Spork's eyes bulged and a big smile spread under his ugly, pink snout. "The best game," he said. "But you are too slow to win."

Spork rubbed his paws together. He ran his tongue over the tops of his teeth. "You should run." He grunted.

"Yes, run," Fleg ordered. "Before I count to trel."

"Hold on," I protested. "What if we don't want to play?"

"Yeah—why should we?" Nat demanded.

"You have to play," Fleg replied. "Read that sign over there."

He pointed to a cardboard sign tacked to one of the gourd trees. The sign read: GAME IN SEASON.

Fleg stared down at me. His eyes narrowed menacingly. His wet nose flared.

He grinned. Not a friendly grin.

"Game in season?" Nat read the sign in a trembling voice.

"You have to tell us how to play," I declared. "I mean, we can't play a game without knowing what it is."

Spork growled deep in his throat and moved closer to me. So close I could smell his fur. What a sour stench!

Fleg reached out a paw and held Spork back.

"It's a good game," Fleg told us. "It's very exciting."

"Uh . . . why is it so exciting?" I asked.

His eyes narrowed. "It's a game of *survival*!" he replied with a grin.

Survival?

Oh, no! *No way* I wanted to play!

"You have until the sun sinks behind the Gulla Willow," Fleg declared.

"What's a Gulla Willow?" Nat asked.

"And where is it?" I wanted to know.

"At the edge of the woods," Fleg replied. He waved a paw to the trees.

"Which edge? Where? How will we know which tree?" I demanded.

Fleg flashed Spork a grin. They both made weird choking sounds in their throats.

I could tell they were laughing. All the other creatures started laughing, too. Such an ugly sound. More like gagging than laughing.

"We can't play the game unless we know more," I shouted.

The laughter stopped.

Spork scratched the bugs on his chest. "It's

simple. If you're It when the sun goes down, you lose," he told me.

The others grunted in agreement.

"And what happens to the losers?" I asked in a trembling voice.

"We nibble on them," Fleg replied.

"Excuse me?" I asked. "You nibble?"

"Yes, we nibble on them. Until dinnertime. Then we eat them."

The creatures around us exploded into more laughter. The sick gagging sound made me feel like puking.

"It's not funny!" Nat shrieked.

Fleg narrowed his eyes at us. "It's our favourite game."

"Well, I don't like your game!" Nat cried.

"We're not going to play. We don't want to," I added.

Spork's eye lit up. "You mean you surrender? You give up?" He smacked his lips hungrily.

"NO!" I shouted. Nat and I jumped back. "We'll play. But by the rules. You have to tell us the rules. All of them."

A cloud rolled overhead. It cast a shadow over the clearing. I shivered.

Were they going to attack us because we didn't want to play?

"Made in the Shade!" Spork cried suddenly.

"Made in the Shade," Fleg repeated.

Huh?

"What's going on?" I demanded.

The cloud slowly passed.

"No time to explain," Fleg said. He waved a paw at the other creatures. "Let's go," he insisted. "This time-out has been too long."

"This isn't fair!" Nat protested. "Please. We need to know the rules."

"Okay," Fleg said as he turned to go. "Gling— you must always attack from the east."

"The east," I mumbled. I raised a hand to shade my eyes as I scanned the clearing.

East. North. South. West. I pictured a map. East was to my right. West to my left. But which direction was east out here in the woods? Why hadn't I listened at that outdoors camp?

'Proo—the brown squares are Free Lunch squares," Fleg continued.

"You mean they're for resting? They're safe?" I asked. I liked that rule. Maybe we could find a brown square and stay there until sunset.

Fleg snorted.

"No. Free Lunch. It means anyone can eat you!" He glared down at me. "Rule Zee," he announced. "You must be three feet tall to play."

I glanced at the beasts. They were at least ten feet tall! So much for Fleg's rules.

"Well, thanks for explaining," I said, shaking my head. "But we really can't play this game. We have to find our parents and—"

"You *must* play," Fleg growled. "You're It. You're the Beast from the East. Play—or surrender."

"The sun will be down soon," Spork added, licking his fang.

"You have until the sun goes down behind the Gulla Willow tree," Fleg said. "Then, the Beast from the East is the loser."

Spork made a choking sound, his ugly laugh. "You will make a delicious loser. I'm thinking maybe a sweet-and-sour sauce. Or perhaps you'd go better with something a little more spicy."

The creatures all gagged and choked. They thought Spork was a riot.

Fleg turned to the woods. He stopped. "Oh," he added with an evil grin. "Good luck."

"Good luck," Spork repeated. He poked a finger into his open eye socket and scratched inside it. Then he turned and lumbered after Fleg.

The other creatures followed. The earth trembled under their heavy feet. In a few moments, the clearing stood empty again.

I gaped at Nat.

This wasn't a game! These evil monsters searched the woods for lost kids. And then they—

"What are we going to do?" Nat cried. "Maybe they've already eaten Pat. Maybe they found him on a brown Free Lunch square."

"And Mum and Dad, too," I murmured.

He let out a frightened gasp.

"There *has* to be somewhere safe!" I told him. "The way we use the porch at home when we play tag."

Nat swallowed nervously. "What's safe here?"

I shrugged. "I don't know," I admitted.

"We can call time-out," Nat suggested. "You're always allowed a time-out in every game."

"This is different. This is for our lives," I said softly.

The leaves rustled in the trees above us. The wind made the gourds whistle.

I heard a low growl. Then a creature laughed. That ugly gagging sound. Twigs crackled. Bushes swayed. I heard low grunts.

"We'd better start playing," Nat urged. "They sound hungry."

"How can we play?" I cried. "There's no way we can win. There are too many of them. And we don't even know where that Gulla tree is."

"So what?" Nat demanded. "We don't have a choice—do we?"

The leaves in a tree branch over our heads rustled. The branch started thrashing around.

Thud.

I shrieked and leaped back.

Something small and brown hit the ground at my feet.

One of those small, brown animals we had seen earlier. It rubbed up against my leg, and made a gurgling sound.

"At least these little guys aren't mean," Nat said. He reached down to pet it.

The animal snapped at Nat's hand, clamping four rows of tiny, sharp teeth.

"Whooa!" Nat jerked his hand away and

leaped back. The animal scurried into the underbrush.

Nat swallowed hard. "Weird," he murmured. "What kind of forest is this? How come there aren't any *normal* animals?"

'Shhh!" I placed my finger over my lips and scowled. "Listen."

"I don't hear anything," Nat complained.

"Exactly," I answered.

The grunts and growls and choking laughter had vanished. The woods were quiet. *Really* quiet.

"Now's our chance!" I cried. "Let's run for it." I grabbed his hand.

"Wait!" Nat cried. "Which way?"

I squinted around the clearing. "Back to the stream," I declared. "We'll try to follow it back to Mum and Dad. Maybe we'll hear their voices along the water."

"Okay," Nat agreed.

We raced across the clearing. We plunged into the woods and pushed through the thick line of trees.

I peered ahead into the forest. "This way!" I shouted, pointing to my left.

"Why?" Nat asked.

"Because," I said impatiently. "I see light through the trees up ahead. That means the woods thin out. There were fewer trees near the stream, remember?"

I hurried on. Nat followed. We ran silently for a while. The trees did begin to thin out. Soon, scraggly bushes dotted the ground.

"There!" I stopped. Nat nearly crashed into me. "Up ahead."

"The stream!" Nat exclaimed. He slapped me a high five.

Excited now, we began to run. We reached the water at about the same time.

"Now what?" Nat asked.

"Let's head left again," I suggested. "The sun was in our eyes when we started. So now we want it on our backs."

Yes! I thought. We were definitely heading back the way we came. All we had to do now was follow the stream back to the right clearing. Back to our parents.

"Stay low," I told Nat. "Try not to make any noise, just in case." In case the beasts were following us. "And keep an eye out for Pat," I added.

I had no idea if Pat was still in the woods or not. I hoped he had made it back to our camp. But he could be anywhere. Maybe hiding somewhere nearby, alone and scared.

Thinking about how scared Pat might be made me feel braver. We had to stay calm so we could help Pat.

Nat and I crouched down. We scooted along the stream, pushing through the umbrella

281

bushes that grew close to the water's edge.

I could still see the silvery-blue fish circling below the surface of the water.

Gazing at the fish, I stumbled. I grabbed at a leaf on an umbrella bush to steady myself. The leaf shredded in my hand. Blue sap smeared over my fingers.

Not again! Another colour. Yellow. Red. And now blue. "Ginger! Come here!"

Nat's cry startled me. I rushed to his side.

Nat pointed to the ground.

I glanced down, afraid of what I would see.

"A footprint," I said, frowning. Then I let out a loud whoop.

Nat's boot rested inside the footprint perfectly. It was exactly the same size as his.

"Pat!" we said together.

"He *has* been here!" Nat cried joyfully.

"Yes!" I shouted. Pat had found his way back to the stream.

"Maybe he's already made it back to camp," Nat said excitedly. "We can follow his footprints."

We started out eagerly. With each step I pictured Mum and Dad and Pat's smiling faces when Nat and I showed up at camp.

Pat's footprints marched along the stream for a while. Then they veered into the woods.

We followed them through the trees and found ourselves on a narrow path. The trees grew closer together here.

Overhead, the sun disappeared from view.

The air grew damp and cold.

I heard a familiar growl.

Right behind us.

The ground shook.

"Beasts!" I screamed. "Run!"

I pushed Nat forward. We sprinted down the path. It curved to the right and then back to the left. I had no idea which direction we were going now.

Branches of trees whipped our faces. I struggled to shove them aside. The trees swayed and shook above our heads. Gourds hit the ground all around us.

Something warm and wet tangled itself around my arm. I yanked free. Another wet thing grabbed me.

Vines.

Thick yellow vines.

Some draped over the branches of the trees, dangling on to the forest floor. Others sprouted from the tree trunks. They wrapped around each other, weaving thick nets from tree to tree.

Some vines stretched across the path. Nat and I had to jump and twist, leaping over the vines in our way.

It was hard work. I could hear Nat breathing hard.

My side ached. My breath came in short, sharp bursts.

I longed to rest. But we couldn't rest. The ground was shaking under our feet. The woods echoed with thunderous cries.

The beasts were coming. And they were gaining on us.

"Watch out!" Nat warned.

I spotted a tangled web of vines strung across the path.

Nat jumped the web. He cleared it. I gathered myself and leaped. I jumped high.

But not high enough.

Vines wrapped around my ankles. I fell to the ground.

More thick yellow vines twisted around my legs. Frantically, I grabbed at them and tried to pull them off.

The vines tugged back.

Hard.

"Nat!" I shrieked. "Help!"

"I'm stuck!" he cried. His voice cracked. "Help me, Ginger!"

I couldn't help him. I couldn't move.

I glanced down at my legs. The vines were tugging tighter and tighter.

Another vine inched around my waist.

I gaped down at it.

What were those shiny things?

Eyes?

"Eyes!" I cried out.

Vines don't have eyes!

And then I realized what I was staring at.
The vines weren't vines.
They were snakes.

I screamed.

"Ginger!" Nat cried behind me. "These aren't vines. They're—snakes!"

"Tell me something I don't know!" I groaned.

The snake around my waist uncoiled and slithered on to my right arm. It was covered with thick scales that felt rough against my bare skin.

I took a deep breath. Then I wrapped my left hand around the snake's body. It was warm.

I yanked hard. Tried to pull it off.

No way.

The snake coiled tighter around my arm. Its hard, cold eyes stared up at me. Its tongue flicked in and out.

I felt something brush against my thigh. I glanced down.

Another snake climbed up my body.

Sweat ran down my forehead.

"Ginger! Help!" Nat wailed. "They're climbing all over me."

"M—me, too!" I stammered. I glanced at my brother. His eyes bulged in terror. He twisted and squirmed, trying to free himself.

The snake around my thigh pulled back its head. And stared at me with those piercing eyes.

The snake around my arm wound tighter and tighter—until my fingers turned numb. It hissed. A long, slow hiss. As if it had all the time in the world.

"They're going to attack!" Nat cried in a strangled voice.

I didn't answer. I felt a wiry tongue flick against my neck.

Cold.

Their tongues were cold.

And prickly.

I squeezed my eyes shut and held my breath.

Don't bite. Please don't bite, I prayed.

A growl disturbed the bushes around us.

"*Grrougggh!*"

Fleg jumped out of the bushes. He stared at Nat and me, his mouth open.

I gasped.

I saw Fleg's eyes bulge in surprise as he spotted the snakes. "Double Snake Eyes!" he called out.

My entire body trembling, I gaped at him in horror.

Double Snake Eyes?

Was that good—or bad?

"Congratulations! Double Snake Eyes!" Fleg cried. He shook his head in wonder. "And you said you never played this game before!"

The snakes tightened around me.

I stared at him. "What are you talking about?" I choked out.

"Twenty points—that's what I'm talking about." The huge beast grunted. "I'd better play harder. Or you're going to win!"

"Who cares about winning!" I screamed. "I can't breathe! Get these snakes off!"

Fleg grinned. "Off!" he screamed with laughter. The folds of skin under his jaw flapped up and down. "That's a good one."

"We mean it," Nat pleaded. "Get them off us!"

Fleg seemed confused. "Why?" he asked. "They might bite you."

"We know!" I screamed. "Help us—please!"

The snakes flicked their tongues against my cheek. My stomach lurched.

Fleg grinned. "If they bite you, you could be awarded a Triple Hisser," he explained. "Worth sixty points."

Points for getting bitten. Some game!

"Forget the points!" I shrieked. "Get—them—off. Now!"

Fleg shrugged. "Okay."

He stepped up to me. Then he pushed a claw under the snake that was coiled around my arm. "You need claws to do this right," he bragged.

Fleg scratched his claw along the snake's skin.

I could feel the snake loosen its grip.

"They're ticklish," Fleg explained. He yanked the snake away and tossed it into the woods.

He tickled the other snake, then pulled it from around my leg. Then he turned to Nat and repeated the same motions, tickling the snakes and prying them loose.

When Fleg was done, he leaped towards the edge of the woods.

I struggled to my feet and rubbed my arms and legs. My whole body itched and tingled. I knew I'd see those snakes in my dreams!

Fleg stuck his furry head out from behind a tree.

"You could have tagged me," he called. "Too bad!"

He opened his mouth in a gagging laugh. Then

he plunged into the woods and disappeared.

My mouth dropped open. I stared after him in disbelief.

"Tag!" Nat cried. "Now I get it. It's just like tag. The rules are easy, Ginger." He turned to face me. "Touch one of the beasts, and you won't be It any more. You won't be the Beast from the East!"

Nat took off, running after Fleg.

"Wait, Nat!" I started after him. I stepped on something hard. I heard a crunch.

Another crunch. I glanced down.

"Nat! Stop!" I screamed. I spotted an orange rock at my feet. I picked it up and hurled it after Nat. "Hey—stop!"

I glanced down at my hand. Orange. My fingers had turned orange where they had grasped the rock.

The rock smacked into a tree trunk. Nat stopped. Whirled around. "What did you do that for?" he cried.

"To stop you," I answered.

"Listen, Ginger," Nat urged. "You have to tag one of the beasts. It's the only way to win the game. To stay alive."

"I don't think so," I said as calmly as I could.

Nat scowled. "What's your problem? It's just like tag."

"No," I said. "This is *not* just like tag. Not the game that we used to play."

I pointed at the ground.

Nat stepped closer. He gazed down to where I was pointing.

He gasped. "What *is* that?" he asked.

"Bones," I murmured. "A pile of animal bones."

Nat and I stared. The bones gleamed coldly in the sunlight. Picked clean.

"Notice anything else?" I pointed to the ground beside the bones.

"What?" Nat frowned.

"It's brown," I said. "The grass under the bones. It's a square brown patch."

Free Lunch.

Nat swallowed hard.

"A beast ate it," he murmured. "Whatever it was."

I wrapped my arms around my chest. "This is not like tag, Nat," I told him solemnly. I couldn't take my eyes off the poor animal's bones. "This game is deadly."

"Only if we lose," Nat said. "Ginger, we just saw Fleg. He helped us."

"So?" I asked.

"So, we'll make him help us again."

"How can we do that?"

Nat grinned. "Easy. We'll trick him. Pretend to need help. Pretend you have another snake on you or something."

"Right," I replied, rolling my eyes. Like I was really going to let Fleg near me again.

Nat grabbed my arm. "It'll work. You scream for help. Fleg gets close. You jump out and tag him. Easy." Nat snapped his fingers.

I shook my head. "Forget it. I'm going to find the stream again and get out of here."

"Why are you so stubborn?" Nat cried.

"Because I'm It!" I screamed. "I'm the one they're going to eat!"

"I-I know we can win if we try," Nat stammered.

I took a few deep breaths and tried to get rid of the panic in my chest.

"Okay," I said finally. "Okay. Okay. I'll try it. What should I do?"

Nat beamed at me. "First I'll climb a tree," he said. "I can spot the beasts' hiding places from up there."

I gazed up at the tall, leafy trees around us.

I thought about it. All we needed was to tag one beast. Any beast.

"Do it," I told Nat. "But don't stay up there too long."

Nat searched the woods for the best tree. "That one," he said finally.

The tree was tall. Dozens of sturdy branches sprang from its sides. In the centre of each branch was a big, strong knot. Tiny golden leaves covered the branches. The tree looked strong, strong enough to hold Nat.

"This is a cinch," he assured me. "As easy as climbing a ladder. I'll be able to see *everything* from up there."

I waited near the base of the tree.

Nat placed his foot on the lowest branch and hoisted himself up.

He climbed slowly. Steadily.

"See anything yet?" I called anxiously.

"I see a weird nest," he shouted down. "With big eggs."

"What about the beasts?" I yelled. "Do you see them?"

"Not yet." Nat climbed higher. A few seconds later, he disappeared from view.

"Nat! Can you hear me?" I called. I cupped my hands around my mouth. "Nat! Where are you? Answer me!"

I rushed around the tree, peering up through the branches. I spotted Nat near the very top.

Nat was moving carefully. He let go of one branch and pulled himself on to the next highest branch. The top of the tree swayed dangerously.

I caught my breath.

Maybe this wasn't such a good idea.

Not if I had to climb up and rescue him.

"Nat!" My throat hurt from shouting so loud. "Be careful!"

The trunk swayed back and forth. Slowly at first. Then faster.

Bits of loose bark broke off and fell in slow spirals towards the ground.

The thick branches swished back and forth. Each branch started to bend in the middle.

At the knots.

I stared. The branches reminded me of something. Something familiar.

Arms, I thought. The knots were like elbows. And the branches were like big arms, reaching . . .

I blinked. Was I seeing things?

The branches *were* reaching.

They were reaching for Nat.

"Nat!" I screamed.

High above me, I saw him grasp on to a slender branch.

"Nat!" I ran frantically around the base of the tree, pounding my fists on the trunk. "Nat! Come down!" I yelled. "The tree is alive!"

Nat peered down at me from the top of the tree. "What's wrong?" he called down.

"Come down!" I screamed. "The branches—"

I was too late.

The upper branches grabbed at Nat's arms. Pinned them to his side. I saw him gasp in shock.

Other branches lashed out, slapping him.

Slapping him. Whipping him.

"Ginger!" Nat screamed."Help me!"

What could I do?

I gazed up in horror as two lower branches reached up towards Nat. The top branches passed him down to the lower branches.

The branches wrapped around him, hugging tight.

This isn't happening! I told myself. This *can't* be happening!

Nat's feet dangled in the air. He kicked furiously at the tree. "Let me go! Let me gooooo!"

More branches lashed out. Some held him tight. Others swiped at him, slapping at him.

The branches passed Nat down.

They were carrying him lower, down to the centre of the tree.

Where the branches were the thickest.

Where the tree's arms were strongest.

Nat cried out. He kicked out again and again. The branches wrapped around his legs.

No way to climb up to him. Every branch was thrashing wildly. Even the little thin ones that couldn't reach Nat were clawing upwards. Straining to take a swipe at him.

As I watched helplessly, the thickest branches pulled Nat into the centre.

He disappeared.

"Help!" His muffled cry drifted down to me. "Ginger—it's going to *swallow* me!"

I had to do something. Had to pull him away somehow. Had to free him from the living tree.

But how?

We had got rid of the snakes. We had to get rid of the branches, too. If only . . .

That's it!

I had a crazy idea. But maybe, just maybe it would work.

If the tree is alive, maybe it has feelings, I thought.

And if it has feelings, maybe it's ticklish— just as the snakes were!

"Ginger! Help!" Nat's cries grew weaker.

I knew I didn't have much time.

I leaped at the tree. A branch dipped down and slapped at me.

I jumped back and scrambled around the trunk. I ducked as a thick branch swung at me.

The tree was trying to keep me away while it swallowed up my brother. But I ducked beneath the slapping limbs and branches.

Reached out. And began to tickle the rough bark.

Tickled it with one hand. Then with both.

Was that a shiver? Did the tree actually shiver?

Or did I imagine it?

Please! I silently begged. Please, please, let go of my brother.

I tickled furiously with both hands. "Nat!" I called. "Nat! Can you hear me?"

Silence.

"Nat? Nat?"

No answer.

I didn't give up. I tickled harder.

The trunk started to jiggle.

Bunches of leaves shook free and floated down. They landed in my hair and covered my arms as I jabbed and scratched at the tree trunk.

I tickled harder. The branches shook and swayed. The trunk wriggled.

Yes! I thought excitedly. It's working! I think it *is* ticklish!

I'll make this tree collapse with laughter!

I tickled harder. The trunk squirmed under my fingertips.

I glanced up. Nat's boots poked through the leaves.

Then his legs. His arms. His face.

The branches were shaking. Quivering and shaking.

Nat swung free. He leaped from branch to branch. His tree-climbing skills were finally coming in handy!

"Hurry!" I shouted up to him. "I can't keep this up much longer. Jump!"

Nat wriggled down the tree trunk.

"Here goes!" Nat cried. He let go of the trunk and leaped into the air.

He landed in a crouched position at my feet. "Whoa! Good job, Ginger!"

I grabbed his hand and we hurtled away from the tree.

Nat brushed twigs and leaves from his hair. "I saw some beasts!"

I bit my lip. In all the excitement over the living tree, I had forgotten we were playing a deadly game.

"I saw three of them," Nat reported. "Fleg, Spork, and another one with a smashed tail. That way." He pointed to the right.

"What were they doing?" I asked.

"They are all hiding behind a big, grey boulder. You can sneak up on them, easy."

"Right." I rolled my eyes. "Piece of cake."

"You can do it." Nat's dark eyes locked on mine. "I know you can, Ginger."

Nat led the way. We crept slowly through the woods towards the boulder.

The sky dimmed overhead and the air grew cooler. I knew that it was nearly evening. Soon the sun would disappear behind the Gulla Willow tree.

I hoped I had enough time.

"There's the rock!" Nat whispered.

I saw a small clearing in the trees. In the middle of the clearing a craggy, grey boulder rose up from the flat ground.

It was big enough to hide a dozen beasts.

My heartbeat quickened.

"I'll hide behind this cabbage plant," Nat said.

He ducked behind the plant. I followed. I wasn't quite ready to face the beasts alone.

I bent down and tightened my bootlace, trying to ignore the fluttering in my stomach.

"Just sneak up on them," Nat whispered.

"Come with me," I begged.

Nat shook his head. "Too noisy if we both go," he said. "It's safer if you go alone."

I knew he was right.

Besides, I told myself, it was pretty easy. The beasts behind the big rock had no idea I was coming. All I had to do was tag one of them.

I felt a thrill of excitement. I could do it.

And the game would be over. We'd be safe.

I took a deep breath. "Ready or not, here I come," I whispered.

I crept towards the boulder. I glanced back. Nat poked his head from behind the cabbage and flashed me a thumbs-up sign.

A few more steps and I'd be at the rock. I held my breath.

The grey rock rose up in front of me.

303

I reached out. My fingers were trembling with excitement.

I leaped behind the rock.

"Gotcha," I cried. "You're It!"

"Huh?"

My hand swiped empty air.

They were gone!

No beasts. Only a pile of broken gourds scattered over the ground.

I blinked in surprise. And scrambled to the front of the rock.

No beasts. They had moved on.

"Nat!" I called. "Nat!"

My brother came jogging to the boulder. "What happened?"

"Nothing happened. They're gone," I told him. "Now what?"

"Hey," Nat snapped. "It's not *my* fault."

I stared at him, feeling totally disappointed. And afraid.

A sharp gust of wind kicked up. I glanced at the sky. Shades of pink streaked overhead. The sun was setting.

My chest tightened in despair.

"It's hopeless," I muttered.

Nat shook his head. "Do you know what we need?" he asked.

"No. What?" I replied.

"We need another plan."

I had to laugh. Nat was such a jerk!

He leaned against the boulder and wrinkled his nose. "What kind of rock is this anyway?" he asked.

"A creepy one," I answered.

Nat peered at the huge rock. "Something's growing on it," he said.

"Well, don't touch anything," I warned.

But telling Nat not to do something only makes him want to do it more.

Nat stuck his finger into a hole in the boulder.

The big rock trembled.

A crack appeared at its top and spread quickly.

Nat pulled his finger away.

"What's happening?" I yelled.

A cloud of grey smoke shot up from inside the boulder.

KERPLOOM!

Nat and I ducked, clapping our hands over our ears.

The explosion roared like a million fire-crackers going off at once.

More grey smoke billowed out of the boulder.

306

I could barely see Nat. I started to cough. My eyes burned.

The smoke filled the clearing around us and drifted above the treetops. A few seconds later, it faded away.

And I saw Fleg standing in the clearing.

Spork appeared behind him, scratching at his open eye socket.

Another beast followed. And then another. They stared at Nat and me.

"You touched the Penalty Rock!" Fleg cried.

Nat took a step closer to me. "Huh?"

Fleg nodded to the beast with the smashed tail. "Get him, Gleeb," Fleg growled.

Gleeb's snout tensed. His eyes bulged. He reached out for Nat's arm.

"Wait! Stop," I yelled. "Nat didn't know it was a penalty."

"Not fair! Not fair!" Nat cried.

The beasts ignored us.

Gleeb scooped Nat up and lifted him high in the air. "Let's go," Gleeb grunted.

Gleeb balanced Nat on both paws. Then he pretended to drop him.

Nat shrieked.

Gleeb and the other beasts snorted their ugly laughter, clapping their hairy paws together.

"Stop it!" I screamed. "Let him go!"

"Yes, go," the beasts echoed. They clapped their paws again. "Let's go! Let's go!" they chanted.

I glared at Fleg. "Tell him to put my brother down."

"He touched the Penalty Rock," Fleg explained. "He must have his penalty."

"But we didn't know about it!" I protested. "We don't know any of your dumb rules. That isn't fair."

I tried to grab Nat's dangling legs.

"Let me see your hand," Fleg demanded. He snatched at my arm and lifted my hand up to his eyes. He studied my palm.

"Nubloff colours!" he exclaimed. He studied me. "That's fifty points. You can't trick me. You've played this game before. You already know the rules."

I stared at my hand. Yellow sap from the stick. Blue from the leaf of the umbrella plant. Orange from the rock. Nubloff colours?

"But . . . but . . ." I stammered. "I didn't get these colours on purpose. They just happened."

Fleg and Spork exchanged glances.

"Come," Fleg ordered, waving to Gleeb.

Gleeb tossed Nat over his shoulder and followed Fleg to the woods. The others stomped after them.

"Ginger!" Nat wailed as the beast carried him away.

I ran after them, feeling totally helpless.

"Stop! Where are you taking him?" I shrieked. "What are you going to do to him?"

I chased after them. Down a wide path lined with more giant rocks.

More penalty boulders?

I stayed in the centre of the path, afraid to touch them.

The beasts stopped at the entrance to a tunnel. It was carved into the side of the largest rock I had ever seen. They ducked their heads and hurried inside.

I followed behind, my heart pounding.

"Ginger!" Nat's cry echoed off the tunnel walls.

The beasts growled and grunted, jabbering in excitement. Some pounded their paws on the ceiling as they moved.

Everything shook. The walls. The ceiling. The ground.

"Nat!" I cried. I couldn't hear my own voice over the noise.

I followed the beasts out of the tunnel and into another large clearing.

"What's *that*?" I gasped.

In the centre of the clearing, a large wooden box hung from a tree. It looked like an enormous bird house. I saw a tiny door on one side.

A sign above the door read: PENALTY CAGE.

Gleeb raised Nat high in the air. He held him up for all the beasts to see and spun him round and round.

Nat screamed.

Spork and the other beasts stomped and clapped.

"NO!" I shouted. "You can't do this!"

"He must go in the box," Fleg declared. "He touched the Penalty Rock. It's in the rules."

Gleeb tossed Nat inside the Penalty Cage. He slammed the door. Fleg dropped a large twig into the rough wooden latch to lock the door.

Nat reached through the slats. "Ginger," he cried. "Get me out of here." The penalty box swung in the air.

"Don't worry, Nat," I called. "I'll get you out." I shivered. He seemed so small and helpless.

"You can't keep him in there for ever," I told Fleg. "When does he get out?"

"When we eat him," Fleg replied softly.

"But I'm the Beast from the East!" I protested. "You said you would eat *me*." I took a step closer to him.

"Players in the Penalty Cage get eaten, too." Fleg snorted in disgust. "Don't pretend you forgot. Everyone knows that. It's a basic rule."

"There must be another way to get him out," I said, edging closer.

"Only if he eats a Free Escape Tarantula," Fleg explained. He scratched the flab under his chin.

"Huh? He has to eat a tarantula?" I demanded, taking another step towards the beast.

Fleg narrowed his eyes. "Don't pretend you don't know *that*," he said, beginning to turn away.

I hurled myself at Fleg's hairy chest.

I slapped him hard.

"You're It!" I screamed. I lifted both fists in triumph. "You're It! I tagged you!"

Fleg raised an eyebrow. "Sorry," he said calmly. "I paused the game. It doesn't count."

"No!" I shrieked. "You can't! You can't keep changing the rules!"

"I didn't. Rules are rules." Fleg reached over me and checked the lock on Nat's cage. It held fast.

"Try again," Spork grunted. "You can always try again."

The rest of the beasts nodded in agreement, grinning and snorting in excitement. They were enjoying themselves. They rumbled away from the clearing.

"Ginger!" Nat cried. He pounded on the box. "Get me out of here!"

I gazed at him in despair. No way could I reach him up there.

He stared down at me through the slats. His brown hair fell into his eyes. "Do something," he pleaded.

"I'll try again," I said.

It was the only thing to do.

"Can you see them?" I called up to him. "Which way did they go?"

Nat pointed. "I see a few beasts hiding over there."

"I'll be back," I promised. "After I tag one of them."

I tried to sound as if it was a sure thing. I wished I could believe my own words.

"Hurry!" Nat called after me.

A strong wind blew through the clearing, rocking the cage from side to side. Nat hunched down, hugging his knees.

I gave him one last look and took off.

Long shadows fell across the ground. I gazed at the sky. The orange was turning into deep pink. Almost sundown.

I plunged into the darkening woods.

All around me I could hear small animals skittering through the carpet of leaves on the forest floor. As if hurrying home before sunset.

Home. Where they were safe.

The wind howled loudly through the trees. I stumbled and almost fell over a rotted tree stump.

The woods were closing in on me. Time was closing in on me.

And then I saw a beast hiding behind an umbrella bush. His shoulders slumped forward. His head bobbed gently up and down.

He was sound asleep.

Here's my chance, I thought.

I moved slowly towards him. The beast shifted position.

I stopped. Held my breath.

He quietened down again. He must have moved in his sleep.

This is it, I thought. My chance. In a second, he'll be the Beast from the East.

I rushed forward.

And gasped.

The earth dropped away.

Nothing under me.

Nothing but air.

I fell quickly. Sank straight down.

Down . . . down . . . down . . .

Screaming all the way.

I hit solid ground.

Hard.

The air burst from my lungs.

My shoulder jammed against a sharp rock.

I cried out. Rubbed my arm.

Struggling to catch my breath, I pulled myself up and stared around me.

Too dark. I couldn't see a thing.

It's over, I thought. The game is over.

"Hey—is anyone up there?" I called. "Can anyone hear me?"

I stopped and listened for an answer. Any answer.

Silence.

I forced myself to my feet. My shoulder ached. I rolled it back and forth a couple of times to keep it from getting stiff.

I reached out and patted the walls around me. Solid dirt. I was in some sort of deep pit. The kind people dig to trap animals.

Now I was the trapped animal.

I ran my hands quickly over the walls. Maybe I could find something to hold on to. Some way to climb out.

Yuck! What was that?

My hand touched something cold sticking out of the side of the pit.

I clenched my teeth and forced myself to touch it again. It stayed firm under my fingers. A root, I thought excitedly.

It's not alive.

I ran my hand further up the wall. The roots were everywhere. As high up as I could feel. Perfect!

I raised my foot and stepped on to the lowest root. It held.

Footholds! I could climb out of the pit.

My hands grabbed the highest root I could reach. I pulled myself up. I heard a crumbling of loose dirt.

I pressed myself against the wall as more dirt sifted down the side of the pit, spraying my face.

I squeezed my eyes shut. Waited for the dirt to stop falling. Then I found the next root and began climbing again.

How much time did I have left? How much time before the sun went down?

My shoulder ached. But I had a long way to go. I rested briefly against the wall. Then I continued climbing.

Snap!

The root shattered under my right foot. My leg dangled in the air.

Snap!

The root under my right hand popped loose.

"Hey!" I cried out as I felt myself fall.

I landed hard on the floor of the pit. I lay still for a moment, trying to catch my breath.

I gazed up. A last bit of pink sky glowed over the mouth of the pit.

In the fading light, I looked around. I saw the useless roots on the sides of the deep hole. I glanced down.

Oh, no.

There was just enough sunlight to see the ground beneath me.

It was brown.

And square.

A Free Lunch square.

I was trapped. Trapped on a Free Lunch square. The beasts could eat me—any time they wanted.

I froze in panic. And heard rumbling footsteps above me.

I huddled in a corner of the pit. Pressed my back against the dirt.

"This way!" I heard Fleg shout. "She's down here!"

Fleg appeared in the opening above me. His flabby chin hung down. His eyes locked on to mine.

"Found you!" he cried.

Spork slid next to Fleg. He grinned down at me and drooled yellow drool. It spattered beside my boot.

"Something down there smells delicious!" Spork cried. "I'm soooo hungry!"

Gleeb shoved his furry face between Fleg's and Spork's.

He smacked his lips. I heard his stomach growl.

"Finally!" Spork grunted. "Pull her out! Let's eat!"

I covered my face with my hands. "Please. Don't hurt me," I cried. "I haven't done anything to you."

Fleg shrugged. "You play the game. Sometimes you win. Sometimes you lose."

Spork and Gleeb reached down into the pit. Their big paws swiped at me.

I pressed my back tighter against the wall. "Please," I begged. "Please go away and leave me alone. You win, okay? You can have all my points."

"Points can't be given away," Fleg scolded. "You know that."

The others grunted in agreement. They reached down for me.

My eyes searched the pit.

I needed a weapon.

The roots?

I yanked a fat one out of the dirt.

"Stay back!" I shouted, whipping the root at their paws.

The beasts slapped each other on the back and laughed their ugly laugh.

"You'll be sorry," I threatened.

Who was I kidding? This stupid root couldn't hurt them. And they knew it. I was the Beast from the East. I was dinner.

Fleg leaned into the pit and snarled. His claws were only inches from my face.

I ducked.

His paw brushed against the back of my neck. I felt claws scratch my skin.

I jerked away. The hair on my arms stood straight up.

If only I could burrow into the earth like an animal, I thought.

Fleg's paw swiped the air in front of my face.

"Stop ducking away," he shouted. "You're just making me hungrier."

"This isn't fair!" I screamed.

He turned to Spork and Gleeb. "I'm tired of this," he complained. "Enough stalling!"

His round eyes gleamed down hungrily at me.

"Get her!" he bellowed.

Spork leaned down and grabbed my arm. I felt his claws dig into my skin. He pulled me up and yanked me to my feet.

It's all over, I thought sadly. The game is over.

A cloud passed overhead, throwing the pit into deep shadow.

Fleg howled. He slapped his broad forehead. "Made in the Shade!" he cried.

Spork opened his paw and let go of my arm.

I dropped to the ground. Fell to my knees.

"Made in the Shade!" Spork cried.

"Made in the Shade!" Gleeb echoed.

I climbed to my feet. The angry voices of the beasts made my head throb.

They stomped their feet loudly.

"What's going on?" I demanded.

"You're safe," Spork replied, sneering in disgust. "This time."

Safe? I breathed a sigh of relief.

"But . . . why?" I asked, amazed.

"You're Made in the Shade," Fleg explained. "We can't touch you. It's a free pass. But you can only use it once."

Once was enough, I hoped. I didn't plan to play this game for ever.

"We have to let you go this time," Fleg growled. "But you're still the Beast from the East."

"You still have to tag someone before sundown," Spork agreed.

Gleeb sighed. The three beasts turned to the woods. "We'll go now," Fleg announced.

"Wait!" I scrambled to my feet. "How do I get out of here? How can I tag someone if I'm stuck in this pit!"

Fleg rolled his eyes. He reached down and pressed one paw against a purple rock on the ground near the edge of the pit.

The pit floor creaked and groaned.

Then it rose up. Higher and higher.

Finally it jerked to a halt a few feet below the ground.

I was close enough to stare at the beasts' ankles. I could see shiny black insects crawling in their fur. I swallowed nervously. Was this some kind of trick? Or was I really safe?

"I still need help to climb out of here," I told Fleg.

Fleg pounded on the purple rock again.

The floor started moving. This time it stopped level with the ground.

I hopped off the Free Lunch square. The beasts circled me.

"The sun is almost down," Fleg warned. "The game is almost over."

"You don't have much time," Spork added.

Fleg snorted. Then he turned and lumbered away.

"Good luck," Spork cried as he hurried after Fleg. Gleeb followed. They raced back towards the stone tunnel.

"Wait!" I yelled. I ran after them as fast as I could.

I raced into the rock tunnel. I could hear the beasts up ahead of me. They growled and grunted, scraping their claws across the walls and ceiling again. Making a racket.

I saw them burst through the other side of the tunnel. They split up, running in different directions.

Which way should I go? I knew I couldn't waste time.

I followed Fleg.

He wove in and out between the trees. He leaped over some scraggly bushes.

I panted, straining to keep up.

Fleg picked up the pace.

Faster and faster.

I could barely keep up now. I was gasping for air.

"Wait!" I shouted desperately. "Wait!"

Fleg glanced once over his shoulder. He disappeared into the trees. I stopped running after him.

Overhead, the sky turned to purple. Soon it would be completely dark.

I spun around, searching desperately for a beast to tag.

"Yoo-hoo! Over here!" I heard a call.

I whirled around.

Spork. He waved to me from between two tall trees.

I raced towards him.

Spork lumbered down a twisting path. I followed him.

What else could I do?

Suddenly, my foot caught on a rock. I sprawled into the dirt.

I forced myself to get up. The woods were quiet around me.

No beasts.

I wanted to scream! So I did.

"Fleg! Spork! Gleeb! Where are you?" I shouted. How could I tag them? I couldn't even find them.

My eyes scanned the area.

What was that? I squinted harder.

Yes! A blue furry head! It popped up behind a bush.

My last chance.

I gathered my energy and sprinted towards the bush.

My hand reached out.

"Tag!" I yelled. "You're—"

"*Gurraugh!*" The tiny beast pawed the air.

The baby beast! The only beast under three feet tall. Too short to play the game.

Not fair! I thought.

My hopes were crushed. Again.

I picked up a rock and heaved it angrily into the woods.

"Where is everyone?" I screamed. "Come out and play!"

The little beast patted its claws together and gurgled happily.

I stared at it. Why was it here all alone?

Then it hit me. Of course.

There must be another beast nearby. A grown-up beast to watch the kid. One over three feet tall.

One I could tag.

I checked out the area. Trees and large rocks. I would have to search behind every one of them.

Taking a deep breath, I tiptoed silently

through the trees. Stopped to peer behind each rock.

Crunch. My foot cracked a pile of twigs.

I stood completely still. And waited.

Silence.

I moved forward.

I listened carefully.

Silence.

I crept forward. A beast had to be here somewhere.

But where?

Then I heard a noise.

Mumbling.

I crept behind a bush and inched closer to the sound. It came from behind a tall, jagged rock.

I peeked out.

Spork!

Yes! Spork stood behind the rock, talking to himself. He scratched the lump scar on his nose.

I could easily tag him.

But was this another penalty rock?

Would it go up in smoke?

I didn't want to end up in a cage dangling above the ground.

Like Nat. Poor Nat.

I took another deep breath and inched closer to Spork.

Spork turned and searched the woods behind him. "Little beast," he called out. "Is that you?"

I dropped to the ground and waited.

326

My heart pounded in my ears. I forced myself to stay quiet.

Spork didn't move from his spot. He sighed and started mumbling again.

Three more steps and I could tag him.

Two more.

I wiped my forehead. One more.

It was too good to be true. Spork had no idea I was behind him.

I smacked him hard. "You're It!" I shrieked.

Spork gasped in surprise. His big paws shot up into the air. I thought he was about to faint!

"I've done it! I've done it!" I cried happily.

I was free!

Nat was free!

Spork grunted and raised himself up. He towered over me. He didn't seem the least bit upset. But he had just lost the game.

"You're It!" I repeated. "You're the Beast from the East!"

Spork raised a paw lazily and scratched his open eye socket.

I felt a chill of fear. What if Spork refused to obey the rules?

"Sorry," Spork said softly. "Not this time."

"Hey—!" I shouted angrily. "You have to obey the rules! I tagged you, fair and square!"

Spork stared at me as if I were being very funny.

Something was wrong.
But what! What was it?
Why didn't he say something?
Spork's lips curled into a nasty grin.

"You tagged me from the west," Spork whispered. "It doesn't count."

I could feel the blood rush to my face. "Not fair! I tagged you! I tagged you!" I wailed.

Spork shrugged.

"You have to tag me from the east. Remember?" Spork's little eyes nearly disappeared as his face crumpled in laughter. "You're *still* the Beast from the East!"

I groaned.

How could I have forgotten? That was the most important rule of all.

How was I supposed to know which way was east? I couldn't even see the sun any more!

My head throbbed. My whole body ached. I was sore and hungry.

Spork stood there, shaking with silent laughter.

I glanced at the darkening sky.

Wait a minute!

I climbed up on the boulder. The sun was setting behind me. That was the west. In front of me was east.

I studied Spork. Without Fleg around, the big beast seemed less menacing. Harmless almost.

After all, he was supposed to be babysitting. And what had happened? He'd lost the little beast.

And now he was so busy laughing at my mistake, he had practically forgotten about me.

"Hey, Spork," I called. "Do you want to play one of *my* games now?"

"But we're still playing this one," Spork blinked in surprise.

"I'll pause it. It's kind of boring anyway, isn't it?" I asked. "My game is lots more fun."

Spork scratched the hole where his eye used to be. He pulled a big, black insect out of it, and tossed the insect away. "What's your game called?"

"Freeze Frame," I answered quickly.

Nat and Pat loved to play this game.

"We spin around and when I say stop, we freeze—and see if one of us can keep our balance and not fall over."

"Sounds fun," Spork agreed. "Why not?"

"Okay then," I said. "Let's try it. Spin!" I shouted.

We both started to spin.

I peeked at Spork. His arms swung out as he whirled around.

"Faster!" I called out. "Much faster."

Spork whirled faster and faster as he turned around in circles.

His tail swished against the bushes. I jumped out of the way.

Spork started to wobble.

"Game—*unpaused*!" I shouted.

Spork didn't seem to hear me. He teetered and stumbled into a tree.

"Freeze!" I shouted.

Spork froze in place.

I leaped at him and tagged him. Hard.

From the east.

"You're It!" I shouted. I backed away. "I tagged you from the east! This time you're really It!"

Spork placed both paws against his head and closed his eyes. I could tell he was still dizzy. He spread his legs and balanced himself against the tree.

He bopped himself in the face with his paw. "You did it," he agreed. He ran his bumpy tongue over his lips. He exhaled a deep breath. "I'm It," he admitted.

"Yes. Yes. Yes!" I cried. I jumped up in excitement.

Spork plopped down against the boulder.

"I'm free!" I shrieked. "The game is over." I

clenched my hand into a fist and pumped my arm.

"I'm going to rescue Nat," I said. "Which way is he?"

Spork pointed his clawed finger to my right.

"We're outta here!" I shouted.

I'd never been so happy in all my life.

"Well, Spork old pal," I said, beaming at him. "This is goodbye. See you!"

"Not so quick," Spork said. "I'm afraid you can't leave."

"Forget it," I said. "You can't change the rules again! No way."

"You can't leave," he repeated. "The game continues until sunset." He glared at me stubbornly.

I gazed at the sky. The purple was fading to grey. Not much time left. But enough.

I wasn't going to be It again.

I could hide until dark. But where?

"Don't just stand there," Spork warned. "You could be tagged again."

"Never," I insisted. "I won't let that happen."

Before I could move, Fleg stomped from behind a tree. The flabby skin under his chin swung from side to side.

Gleeb crept behind him.

"She tagged me!" Spork told them.

"I knew it!" Fleg stared at me. "I knew you'd played this game before."

I clenched my hands into fists. I was angry. I'd had enough.

They forced me to play their stupid game. But I wasn't going to lose now.

Fleg waved me away. "You have until I count to trel," he said. "Then we're allowed to come after you again."

He turned his back and covered his eyes. "Gling ... proo ... zee ... freen ... trel," he counted.

I had no choice. I ran.

Don't stop, I told myself. Don't think about anything. Run. Find a place to hide.

"Ready or not—here we come!" I heard Fleg cry.

Behind me, the beasts growled and grunted in excitement.

I hurled myself off the path and pushed through the tall, scratchy grass between the trees. I jumped over a clump of cabbage plants.

My legs ached. My feet burned.

But I couldn't stop.

Not until I reached a hiding place.

I skidded to a stop when I heard rushing water. I nearly fell into the stream. A large blue fish leaped out of the water and snapped at my ankles.

This was no place to hide. I turned back into the woods.

A cold wind blew in my face. The gourds whistled their strange melody.

"Here I come!" Spork shouted off to my left.

I pushed myself faster. No way he was getting to tag me.

I glanced around. Which way?

The rock tunnel! I saw it only a few feet away.

I darted into the darkness. Without the beasts yelling and shouting, it was eerily quiet inside. I slowed down and tiptoed through the tunnel.

When I reached the other side, I crept into the dense trees. I slumped against a tree and waited, trying to keep quiet. I was breathing so hard I was afraid the beasts could hear me!

A moment passed.

I felt the trembling that meant the beasts were approaching.

I held my breath and ducked beneath an umbrella plant.

Seconds later, Fleg, Spork and Gleeb burst out of the tunnel and raced down the path. Four more beasts followed behind them. They passed the bush where I was hiding. Crashed into the woods. And kept going.

I waited to make sure they were gone.

Silence.

I breathed a sigh of relief.

I scrambled to my feet and stretched.

Something rushed at me from behind.

"No!" I cried in terror.

Two arms wrapped around my waist. And a creature threw me to the ground.

I thrashed and kicked wildly.

"Stop it. Cut it out!" a familiar voice demanded.

"Nat!" I screamed. I whirled around. "Nat! You're safe! How did you get out of the cage?"

"Cage? What cage?" My brother squinted at me.

"The penalty cage," I declared. "Nat—how did you escape? Did they let you go?"

"I'm not Nat. It's me, Pat."

"Pat?" I stared at him in confusion. Then I threw my arms around his neck. I'd never been so happy to see him.

"Where have you been?" I demanded.

"Where have *I* been?" Pat cried. "Where have *you* been? I've been searching everywhere for you guys. These woods are creepy."

He glanced around. "Where's Nat, anyway?"

"Trapped." I started to explain. "See, the

beasts got him. After you ran into the woods, we had to play this game and . . ."

"A game?" Pat cried. He shook his head in disbelief. "I was lost in the woods—and you two are playing a game?"

"It's not what you think," I said.

I checked the trees around us for any sign of the creatures.

"They forced us to play," I told Pat, lowering my voice to a whisper. "It's like tag—only they play for keeps. I was the Beast from the East and—"

"Right." Pat rolled his eyes.

"Really," I insisted. "This game is deadly. You have to believe me."

"Why?" Pat shrugged. "You never believe me. Why should I believe you?"

"Because if we lose, they'll *eat* us!" I told him.

Pat burst out laughing.

"I'm serious!" I grabbed Pat's shoulders and shook him hard. "I'm telling the truth! It's dangerous here. Fleg and Spork are after me, right now."

Pat twisted out of my grasp. "Right. Fleg and Spork. Woof woof!" Pat barked.

"Shhh," I hissed. "Keep quiet!" I pulled him behind an umbrella plant. "Pat, you have to believe me. They're all around us. They could get us if we're not careful."

"And I suppose this game was their idea?" he asked.

"Yes," I answered.

"And I suppose they can talk," Pat went on. "In English."

"Yes. Yes. Yes," I insisted.

"You're weirder than I thought," Pat said, shaking his head. "So where's Nat? For real?"

"*Grrraugh!*"

A deep growl echoed off the nearby rocks. "This way!" A beast bellowed. "Near the tunnel!"

Heavy footsteps pounded closer. The ground shook under our feet.

Pat's eyes widened in shock. He reached for my arm.

"It's them!" I exclaimed. "*Now* do you believe me?"

Pat swallowed hard and nodded his head. "Yes. I believe you," he choked out.

"She's over here!" a beast shouted.

"He heard us," I whispered in Pat's ear. "Run!"

Pat and I took off.

We raced through the woods, leaping over fallen logs, pushing sharp branches out of our faces.

"This way!" I called. I grabbed Pat's hand. "Stay low."

We ducked into a thick clump of trees.

Spork thudded past us.

I could hear him sniffing the air.

"Can he smell us?" Pat asked in a whisper.

"Sshh!" I pressed my finger to my lips.

We crept between the bushy plants.

Fleg appeared, stomping in our direction.

I dropped to my hands and knees. I pulled Pat down beside me.

Fleg thudded past us.

I knew we weren't safe. More beasts would follow. And one of them might find us.

I motioned for Pat to follow me.

We scrambled deeper into the woods.

The trees were close together here. The bushes were so thick I couldn't see between them. I flung out an arm, feeling my way.

My hand brushed against something.

Something big.

And warm.

And furry.

I leaped back. Crashed into Pat.

What had I touched?

The bushes parted and a strange creature bounced out.

I had never seen anything like it.

It had the body of a dog, as big as a German shepherd, and the face of a squirrel.

I don't believe this! I thought.

It could talk, too. "In here! Quick!" the creature urged in a scratchy, squeaky voice.

Its squirrel-nose twitched. Its bushy dog tail thrashed from side to side.

Could we trust it?

"In here!" it squeaked.

It waved a paw in the air. Pointed to a bush of big orange leaves.

Pat held back, but I crept forward. I spotted the entrance to a cave hidden behind the leaves.

"It's a good hiding place," I told Pat.

"It's the Hiding Cave," the squirrel-dog

announced. "The Hiding Cave is the place to hide. Quick!" The animal held the leaves aside for us.

The ground shook. I turned and saw furry blue beasts in the distance. They were moving quickly towards us.

"Better do it, Pat," I said.

Pat hesitated.

I yanked his hand and pulled him after me. I bent down to enter the Hiding Cave.

I suddenly remembered what happened when Nat touched the penalty rock. The thought made me shiver. Would we really be safe in the Hiding Cave?

Thump. Thump.

The beasts drew closer.

Pat hesitated and held back.

"Where are they?" a beast shouted. I recognized Fleg's voice.

"They must be nearby," Spork answered.

The squirrel-dog stayed outside. It let go of the orange leaves. They sprang back into place, hiding the entrance to the cave.

Pat and I crouched inside, hidden from view.

We huddled close together. The air felt damp inside. It had a sour smell that I tried to ignore.

I slumped against the wall of the cave and wiped the sweat off my forehead. I tucked my feet under me. "Try to get comfortable," I whispered to Pat. "We might be here for long time."

Something tickled my neck. I reached to scratch it.

Something tickled my ear.

I shivered.

I brushed my hand against my ear and felt something crawl on to my neck.

"Ow!" I cried out as I felt a sharp bite on my shoulder.

I turned to Pat. He was slapping at his ears and neck.

Something buzzed past my ear.

Something skittered through my hair. I shook my head hard.

My whole body itched and tingled. Every inch of me!

Beside me, Pat squirmed, and wriggled, scratched and slapped at himself.

I leaped to my feet. "Help!" I cried. "What is happening? What is going on in here?"

"Help!" I cried, scratching desperately. "Help us!"

The squirrel-dog's face poked into the entrance.

"What is happening to us?" I cried, squirming and scratching.

"I forgot to tell you," the strange creature whispered. "The Hiding Cave is also a hiding place for insects!"

Insects!

"Ohhh!" Pat let out a low moan. He rubbed his back against the cave wall. Scratched his hair.

The insects were everywhere. Crawling on the walls. Flying through the air. Buzzing. Whistling. Clicking.

They crawled up and down my legs and arms. Over my face. In my hair.

I picked some kind of worm off my cheek. I dragged my hand down my arms and my

344

bare legs, brushing insects on to the cave floor.

Pat squirmed next to me. "Get them off me, Ginger," he wailed. "Helllp!"

"Sshhh!" The squirrel-dog stuck his nose back into the cave. "Quiet! Here comes the Beast from the East. Don't make a sound or he'll find you!"

Pat and I drew closer together.

I held my breath and tried not to move.

I counted to ten. Silently. I pretended there were no bugs on me.

I shut my eyes and pictured my bedroom. The posters on the wall. My comfortable canopy bed. I thought of being under the covers. Going to sleep.

And then I thought about bedbugs!

I couldn't ignore the insects crawling over me. It was impossible not to think about them.

I couldn't stand it. I needed to scratch. I needed to *scream*!

I couldn't sit there another second.

I heard a beast stomp close to the cave opening.

I recognized Spork's voice. "Hey—!" he snarled at the squirrel-dog. "Have you seen strangers here?"

Did Spork know this creature?

Were they friends?

"Answer me," Spork demanded.

I waited for the squirrel-dog's answer. Please

don't tell them we're hiding in here, I prayed. Please.

A fat, wet insect landed on my face. I picked at it with my fingers. It clung to my cheek. I pulled harder. I couldn't tug it loose.

I felt a scream building up inside me.

I couldn't take it another second.

My mouth opened.

I had to scream. I had to!

"Ah—"

I clamped my hand over my mouth.

I let out a tiny squeak.

The orange leaves rustled. Fleg's paw pushed into the cave entrance.

I froze. I heard Pat gasp.

"What's in there?" I heard Fleg ask the squirrel-dog.

"Insects," the squirrel-dog replied. "Thousands of them."

Millions! I thought bitterly. The insects crawled over my face, my arms, my legs. They buzzed in my ears.

Fleg pushed his nose into the cave.

I stopped breathing.

Fleg sniffed. "What's that awful smell?" he complained.

"Insects," I heard the squirrel-dog answer.

"They stink!" Fleg muttered. He let go of the leaves and they snapped back into place. "Only insects in there," Fleg reported to Spork. "No humans."

"Of course not," the squirrel-dog said calmly. "The humans went the other way."

"Why didn't you say so?" Fleg exploded.

Spork shouted to the other beasts. "They're not here! The other way, quick! Only trel minutes left to play."

"I'll find her," I heard Spork tell the others. "I have to tag her back! No human is going to make *me* Beast from the East!"

I heard their footsteps pound in the other direction.

Only trel minutes! I didn't exactly know what trel meant. But I knew the game was nearly over. If Spork didn't tag me back, my brothers and I would be free!

But I couldn't take another second in this insect-infested cave.

I moved to the entrance on trembling legs. I itched so badly, I could barely control my muscles!

I peered out of the cave. "Are they all gone?" I whispered to the squirrel-dog.

"For now," he answered.

"Let's get out of here!" I called back to Pat. I sprang out of the cave. He jumped out after me.

We frantically brushed insects off our skin and clothes. I scratched my head and rubbed my back up against a tree.

348

Pat stomped his feet. "They're even in my boots!" he wailed. He untied his laces and pulled off his boot. He shook it upside down. A hundred black insects poured on to the ground and scurried away.

"I'm never going to stop itching!" I wailed. "I'm going to itch for the rest of my life!"

"You'd better hide," the squirrel-dog warned. "They could be back. And you're only allowed to use the Hiding Cave once a game."

Pat and I thanked the strange creature. Then we plunged back into the woods.

I hadn't been in this part of the forest before. Pat and I pushed our way past a row of high bushes. I stopped.

A giant willow tree stood up ahead. Its branches spread low, sweeping against the ground.

The Gulla Willow?

It had to be.

I glanced around, searching for a hiding place. A long, low rock stretched beyond the tree.

Only a few minutes left.

"Quick," I whispered, grabbing Pat. I pulled him behind the rock.

"That must be the Gulla Willow," I told him. "When the sun sets behind it, we'll be safe."

Pat nodded but didn't reply. He was breathing hard. He scratched his cheeks. Still itchy. We were both still itchy.

"Stay down," I warned him. "And don't touch the rock."

We crouched together in silence.

And waited.

My heart slammed against my chest. My skin tingled. I huddled beside my brother—and listened.

Silence.

The whisper of the wind through the trees. No other sound.

"Are we safe now?" Pat asked in a trembling whisper.

"Not yet," I answered. I raised my eyes to the charcoal grey sky. A last ray of purple light spread over the top of the willow.

Hurry! I urged the sun. Go down! What are you waiting for?

The sky darkened. The purple light faded behind the Gulla Willow.

Only grey sky now. Night sky.

The sun was down.

"We're safe!" I cried, jumping to my feet. I turned and hugged Pat. "We're safe! We made it."

I stepped out from behind the rock.

A heavy hand slapped me hard. On the shoulder.

"You're It!" Spork bellowed. "You're the Beast from the East!"

"Huh?"

I gasped in shock. I could still feel the beast's stinging slap on my shoulder.

"Not fair!" Pat cried. "Not fair!" He stared as the beasts circled us. Pat had never seen them close-up before.

"It's dark! The sun is down!" I protested. "You can't tag me now!"

"Game Over! Game Over!" Fleg shouted. He stepped out of the woods and hurried towards the circle of beasts.

I pointed angrily at the Gulla Willow. "The sun set behind the tree. You can't tag me!"

"The game hadn't been called yet," Spork said calmly. "You know the rule. Fleg has to shout out 'Game Over' before the game can end."

The beasts all murmured agreement.

I clenched my fists. "But ... but ..." I stammered. I lowered my head in defeat. I knew they wouldn't listen to me.

351

Pat gulped. "What will they do now, Ginger?" he whispered softly. "Will they hurt us?"

"I already told you," I whispered back. "They're going to eat us."

Pat let out a cry. He started to say something. But there wasn't time.

Fleg stepped forward and grabbed me by the waist. He tossed me over his shoulder.

The blood rushed to my head and I felt dizzy. The ground was so far away!

Spork hoisted Pat over his shoulder.

"Hey—whoa!" I protested. "Put my brother down!"

"He was your Helper," Spork replied. "We always eat the Helper, too!"

"Put me down!" Pat shrieked. "Let me go."

But the huge beast ignored him.

They carried us both into a small clearing.

A large stone pit sat in the centre. A raging fire burned inside the pit. Yellow and blue flames leaped at the sky.

Fleg lowered me on to a tree stump. Spork set Pat down beside me.

The beasts circled around us. Drooling. Licking their lips.

I thought I heard thunder. But I soon realized it was the sound of their stomachs growling.

"It's Flelday," Spork said, smiling. "On Flelday we always barbecue."

I swallowed hard. And stared at the flames

leaping against the sky. I wrapped my arms around my chest and hugged myself.

Spork poked at the fire with a long metal rod.

He pointed the rod at me. "Yum yum." He grinned, rubbing his stomach.

I felt sick.

Gleeb lugged a huge pot over to the fire. He set it down in the middle of the flames.

Fleg pulled some gourds off the nearby trees. He cracked them open and poured their yellow juice into the pot. He collected sticks and leaves and tossed them in, too.

Gleeb stirred and stirred. A sour, rotting stench rose up from the pot.

"The broth is ready," Gleeb announced.

I turned to Pat. "I'm sorry," I said in a trembling voice. "Sorry I lost the game."

"I'm sorry, too," he whispered, his eyes on the flames.

The beasts began chanting. "Flelday. Flelday. Flelday."

"Who brought the barbecue sauce?" Spork asked. "I'm starving!"

Fleg lifted me in his arms. And carried me towards the cooking pot.

"Whoa! Wait! Stop!"

A familiar voice shouted across the clearing.

I jerked my head around. "Nat!" I screamed.

"Ginger!" Nat cried. He ran towards us, waving his arms. "What's going on? What are they doing?"

Fleg lowered me to the ground. "Nat—!" I screamed. "Run! Find help! Hurry!"

He stopped halfway across the clearing. "But, Ginger—"

"They'll eat you, too," I shrieked. "Run!"

"Capture him!" Spork shouted to the other beasts.

Gleeb and several others took off after Nat.

Nat spun around. He darted for the woods and disappeared into the trees.

I watched helplessly as the beasts plunged into the woods after him.

Don't find him, I prayed, crossing my fingers. All ten of them!

Nat will escape, I told myself. He'll climb a tree. He'll get away from them. Then he'll run and find help.

Pat and I stared at the dark trees. And waited.

"Oh, nooo!" I uttered a long wail when the beasts returned from the woods. And one of them carried Nat over his shoulder.

Nat kicked and punched. But he couldn't free himself.

The beast dumped Nat beside Pat and me. Nat landed hard, face-down on the ground.

Now they had all three of us. A feast!

Spork and Fleg gazed at us hungrily. Gleeb ran his tongue over his long fang.

I dropped down beside Nat. "How did you get out?" I asked him. "How did you get out of that cage?"

Nat rolled over and sat up. "It wasn't that hard," he said, groaning. "The boards were weak. I worked and worked—until I pushed enough boards out. Then I broke out."

"You should have stayed away," I told him. "You should have run. Now they're going to eat you, too."

Nat raised his eyes to the cook pot and the blazing fire. "I—I don't want to play any more," he stammered.

"Nat," I whispered sadly, "I'm afraid the game is just about over."

"Quiet!" Fleg demanded. "Dinner—stop talking!" He stared at Nat.

Fleg's eyes narrowed. He tilted his head. He whispered to Spork and Gleeb.

The other beasts moved closer. They were all moving their eyes from Pat to Nat. They began murmuring to each other, shaking their big, furry heads. Their snouts waved up and down as they talked.

"You doubled!" Spork said to Pat. "You did a Classic Clone!"

I stared at the beasts. Studied their startled expressions. Hadn't they ever seen *twins* before?

"You doubled yourselves!" Fleg declared. "That's a Classic Clone. Why didn't you tell us?"

"Uh . . . tell you *what*?" I asked.

Fleg glared at me. "Why didn't you tell us that you are Level Three players?"

My brothers and I exchanged confused glances.

"You're in the wrong game," Spork announced, shaking his head.

"If you can double yourselves, that means you belong in Level Three," Fleg said. He slapped his furry forehead. "I'm so embarrassed! Why didn't you tell us sooner?"

"Well, I *told* you we didn't want to play," I replied sharply. "But you wouldn't listen."

"I'm so sorry," Fleg apologized. "We're only Level One players. We're just beginners. We're not experts like you."

"Experts?" Pat muttered. He turned to me and rolled his eyes.

"That's why we have to play in the daytime," Fleg explained. "We're not ready to play at night."

All around us, the beasts were muttering and shaking their heads.

"Of course, we'll have to let you go now," Fleg said. He scratched at his flabby chin.

"Well, of course," I cried. I wanted to jump up and down and shout for joy. But somehow I kept myself in control.

"That's it?" Nat cried to Fleg. "We're free?"

"Yes. Goodbye." Fleg scowled. He rubbed his belly. I heard it growl.

"Don't ask again," I told Nat. "Let's just get out of here!"

"Goodbye," Fleg repeated. He waved his paws as if he were trying to shoo us away.

357

I jumped to my feet. I didn't feel tired or scared or itchy or dirty any more.

This time the game was really over!

"How do we find our parents?" I asked.

"That's easy," Fleg replied. "Follow that path." He pointed. "Follow it through the trees. It leads back to your world."

We shouted goodbye—and took off. The narrow dirt path twisted through the trees. Silvery moonlight danced over the ground.

"I am so glad you guys are twins!" I exclaimed.

I had *never* said that before! But I really meant it. They had saved our lives!

The trees thinned out. I could see a full moon climbing up over the dark treetops. I felt as if we were running to it, running into its warm, white light.

"Mum and Dad will never believe this story," I said. I planned to tell them every gory detail.

"They *have* to believe us," Pat declared. "It's all true."

I put on a burst of speed. My brothers ran harder to keep up with me.

I couldn't wait to get back. Mum and Dad must be so worried.

"Oh!" I gasped and skidded to a stop.

Pat and Nat stumbled into me. All three of us struggled to stay on our feet.

A huge beast had stepped out from behind a tree, blocking the path.

He crossed his furry arms over his enormous chest. His snout flared as he stared down at us with cold marble eyes. He opened his lips and growled, exposing his long fang.

I wasn't afraid. Not this time.

"Step aside," I ordered him. "You have to let us go by. My brothers and I are Level Three players."

"You're Level Three? Hey—that's great! So am I!" the beast exclaimed. "Tag! You're It."